A BIT OF WITCHCRAFT

A BIT OF WITCHCRAFT

IRIS GOTCHI

BLOOMSBURY

First published in Great Britain 1989
Copyright © 1989 by Iris Gotchi

Bloomsbury Publishing Ltd, 2 Soho Square, London W1F 5DE

British Library Cataloguing in Publication Data
Gotchi, Iris
A bit of witchcraft.
I. Title
823′.914[F]

ISBN 0-7475-0336-2

Photoset by Rowland Phototypesetting Ltd
Bury St Edmunds, Suffolk
Printed and bound in Great Britain by
Butler and Tanner Ltd, Frome and London

It's World War II in Boring, whoops, Baring-in-the-Marshes. Elfie is eight and her most favourite person is 12-year-old Shonna. But Shonna prefers finding out about witchcraft, how babies are made, and the intricacies of her father's affair with Nora Adora. As the witchcraft and sexual revelations grow in potency, Elfie struggles to understand what is happening around her; an unexpected climax signals her enlightenment into the adult world.

Iris Gotchi's cunning first novel explores the darker side of childhood, where innocence is swallowed by knowing manipulation, with a dextrous black humour and an acute ear for children's speech, which builds a picture of war-torn Britain that would be hard to surpass without a bit of witchcraft.

ACKNOWLEDGMENTS

Among those who have helped and encouraged me, thanks must go to all my family, Nigel Gray and my friends at Leicester University Centre, Kate and Mike Petty, and Jenny Parrott, with a special mention for Debbie Parsons, who unearthed the *Chronicle* for me.

If then all that worldlings prize
Be contracted to a rose;
Sweetly there indeed it lies,
But it biteth in the close.

George Herbert

I

Shonna climbed up on the wooden lavatory seat and drew the black-out curtain across the slit window, shutting out the light from the midsummer moon. Only her toes showed below the hem of her nightie. The three girls gathered around her and shivered in the chill air of the outside toilet. It was June but they wore coats, even though Margaret's and Molly's legs were bare.

'Are you sure your dad won't come out and catch us?' Elfie quivered as the terrifying figure of Mr Creavy, beetle-browed and six foot tall, loomed up in her mind.

'Don't be stupid. It's Friday. He's fire-watching up the High Street,' Shonna hissed. 'Quick. Light the candle.'

Elfie fumbled and dropped the box of matches on the floor, causing Shonna to look round, trip on her nightie and splash one foot down the lavatory pan.

'Shit.' The forbidden word slid from her childish lips with surprising ease as she extricated her foot and looked from one to the other to see the effect it had on them. The girls gasped. Shonna was always so daring, such fun. She jumped down quickly and groped, like someone playing blindman's buff, for Elfie in the gloom, found her soft middle and pinched it viciously with one hand whilst locating the matches with the other. Margaret, crouching down to tie her shoelace, found Shonna's rear end in contact with her nose.

'Get your bum out my face.' Margaret gave her a little push, but Shonna was taking no notice of her; her eyes were fixed on Elfie.

'Now do just one more thing wrong,' Shonna hissed, 'and you'll never come here again. Cross my heart and hope to die.' She marked out the sign between the points of her tiny developing breasts, and then turned and lit the candle, illuminating their faces in its opalescent glow. Elfie, small, fair and rather plump, felt tears forming in her eyes. Margaret, dark, beaky-nosed, suspicious-looking, held hands with her younger sister Molly, who was peering at the scene from behind round pebble-lenses, yawning widely at the lateness of the hour with no idea at all why she was there. According to Elfie's mother, Molly was not quite twelve pence in the shilling.

Shonna looked at them in contempt. What an audience. She knew that she deserved better, and slammed the lavatory seat in a temper, making them jump in the broken silence. From behind the pedestal she produced a small flat earthenware dish filled with nuggets of charcoal, dusted by a yellowish powder. Striking another match, she applied it to the dish and snuffed out the candle. Immediately a tongue of blue flame shot upwards in the darkness, and the unpleasant smell of burning sulphur filled the air. Little Molly squealed loudly and Shonna reached out and clapped her hand over the child's slack mouth, pressing the stubby nose even further upwards.

Margaret stepped forward defensively and prised the hand off. 'Don't you go hurting her. She ain't done nothing.' Margaret's long nose twitched with annoyance.

'Why did you bring her then? I told you it was just for us.' Shonna put her angry face close to Margaret's. In the confined space of the lavatory, they jostled each other with elbows and knees.

'I couldn't get out wivout her. We sleeps in the same bed.

If she woke up and howled for me, Mum would find out and I'd be leathered.'

'Well keep her quiet then.' Shonna held out her hand. 'Give me the rose. Hurry up or it'll get past midnight and the spell won't work.'

The blue flame had settled down now to an eerie glow. Genie-like it hovered over the bowl. Margaret let go of Molly and fished in a crumpled paper bag she was holding, bringing out a wilting tea-rose and put it in Shonna's hand. She took it grudgingly and inspected it.

'Are you colour blind or something? I said a blood red rose, freshly picked from the garden.'

'We ain't got a garden. Ain't no roses in our backyard. If you're so fussy you should have got it yourself. I pinched it from the churchyard. You'll have to make do.'

Shonna clutched the stem, pricking herself on a thorn. She squeezed her finger and a single drop of blood fell and spluttered on the dish. She sucked it quickly and held the rose over the blue glow where it changed colour in the phantom light to a smoky silver.

'Oh! Isn't it pretty?' Elfie gasped. 'Look it's steaming.'

The rose had started to smoke and curl at the edges. Shonna quickly removed it from the heat and placed it still smouldering on the lavatory seat. Then she drew from her nightgown pocket a sheet of white paper sealed with three blobs of red wax.

'On here I have written the initials of myself and my lover. Now I shall take the rose and the paper and bury them under the hawthorn bush in the field,' Shonna solemnly intoned.

'It says in the book,' Elfie interrupted, 'that you must bury it under the bush you took the rose from.'

Shonna looked at her crossly. 'What do you want me to do? Dig up the graveyard at midnight? You know this rose has got to be dug up again on the sixth of July. It says so in the book. I've got to sleep with it under my pillow.' She sighed dramatically and put her hand on her heart. 'Then my dreams will tell me great things for myself and my lover.'

'You ain't got no lover. You're too young. Lovers are for grown-ups.' Margaret was not impressed.

Shonna ignored her, said 'Shh!' and placed a finger on her lips. She picked up the rose and the paper, jerked her head in the direction of the garden, and then set off down the path, leading the way with the fiery dish.

'What if a German plane sees us and drops a bomb?' Elfie was sure it was wrong to show a light during blackout hours.

'They don't drop bombs here. Only on Coventry.' Shonna darted heedlessly through the gap in the hedge to the field behind her house. There, with the three girls huddled round her, she knelt on the damp grass and dug a shallow hole with a trowel she had previously hidden in the weeds. Placing her treasures in it carefully she covered them with the soil, before raising her hands above her head, palms down and chanting in a terrible voice:

'Deirdre Deirdre, drear drah and dree
The man I shall marry, in dreams let me see.'

Elfie looked over her shoulder fearfully, half expecting someone to jump out of the bushes. Margaret gave a nervous giggle, stifling it behind the back of her hand, and pulled at Molly who was scrabbling about in the dirt. They stayed still, watching Shonna, their feet getting colder. It seemed as though she was going to stay there forever. Then Margaret sniffed loudly and wiped her nose on her frayed coat cuff. 'Well? What happens now?'

Shonna did not answer. She kept her face turned up to the moon, eyes closed as though in prayer.

'Doesn't she look pretty?' Elfie whispered to Margaret. 'Like one of those cherubs in the paintings in church. The ones with the rosy cheeks and red curls. She ought to walk around like that always. When her eyes are open she scares me a bit, cos they look like the goblin's beads.'

'What goblin?' asked Margaret, puzzled. She had never seen a goblin wearing beads. They had beards and funny little hats, but no beads. She realized that nothing else was going to happen, took Elfie and Molly by the hand, and led them back towards the house. On an impulse, Elfie's eyes slid upwards and she saw the pale oval of Mrs Creavy's face behind an upstairs window, half hidden by the curtains, as though she did not want to be seen. She was looking out across the field where they had buried the rose. Would Shonna get into trouble? She did not seem to worry if she was late home, and never, ever told her mother where she was going. Elfie, who was supposed to be in before dark, shivered at the thought of what might happen to her if she was caught, but that was all part of the fun. Margaret interrupted her thoughts. 'What was all that old rubbish she was jabbering? Who's that Deirdre person?'

Elfie wanted to impress Margaret with her knowledge, but was not quite sure either. 'I think she's the patron saint of Scotland. Shonna is praying to her cos she's Scottish you know. Her mother is the seventh child of a seventh child and has second sight. She can see things that we can't. Shonna says she can see into the future.'

'Perhaps that's why she's crying at the window,' said Margaret. 'Seen summit she don't like, I'll be bound.'

So Margaret had seen her too. How did she know Mrs Creavy was crying? To Elfie her face had just looked like a pale blur. Perhaps Margaret was making that bit up to get even with her for knowing about the second sight. Margaret never liked to be outdone.

'Did you really see her crying? Did you see the tears?' Elfie asked. But Margaret just said, 'Come on, hurry up. Molly's tired.' She pulled them both behind her down the length of Arcadia Road, which was long, with the best houses at the wide, park end, and tapering away to the Council houses where Margaret and Molly lived. Elfie's house was about half-way down.

Margaret looked back and nodded in the direction of the field. 'She's stupid. Don't she know you mustn't get the new moon on your face. You get moonstruck and then you're a prey to any dark and hairy beast that takes a fancy to you. Werewolves get hold of moonstruck people.'

'Oh,' said Elfie, fearfully. It was nice to be frightened when you were safely holding Margaret's hand.

Half-way along the road they saw Mr Creavy coming from the direction of the town, returning from his fire-watching shift. Elfie shrank towards the fence of the nearest house trying to become invisible. She thought I bet he'll pounce on us and take us home. My mother will have a fit. She thinks I'm asleep in bed. She loosed herself from Margaret's hold and flattened herself against the hedge, holding her breath. Mr Creavy walked past without speaking. He even averted his eyes as though he did not want to see them.

'He ain't been fire-watching at all,' said Margaret in a disgusted voice.

'How do you know?' said Elfie. Was Margaret pretending to have second sight too?

'Cos he ain't got his helmet,' Margaret replied practically, pushing Elfie in through her garden gate. 'Don't make a noise, and don't forget to bolt the door.' Then Margaret hitched Molly up in a piggy-back to carry her the rest of the way home. They looked to Elfie like a St Christopher medal as they disappeared into the darkness heading for home, where the trim gardens gave way to barren front areas of cracked paving slabs, and there were no privet hedges to hide you, and you did not have to worry too much about being seen.

In the week before the sixth of July, Elfie thought of nothing but the rose. It occupied her waking thoughts, delicate and shimmering over the blue flame, and she wished that she could live the whole night over again. She dreamed that Shonna told her who the lover was . . . and what they did together. Perhaps one day she would bury a rose herself and have a life of her own without being part of Shonna's. Elfie imagined what her own lover would look like. He might be a bit like Peter Collins from Lincoln Street, who had lovely soft brown eyes, like a pony. Even if he did bite his nails he might have to do, as she did not know many boys. They had to leave the Convent at nine years old, before any developing male characteristics could disturb the girls. She was not too sure either what one did with a lover, but Shonna would know. She was nearly four years older, and she had the book.

That book figured largely in Elfie's life. Fat and black, it sat on the dresser in Shonna's kitchen and contained in its closely printed pages the answers to almost everything she wanted to know. It was the *News Chronicle's* publication *Everything Within*, a household bible full of useful information. Shonna read to them out of it every Saturday when her mother went shopping. Last week it had been a piece about how to tell the character of your lover by looking at his feet. Men who walked on their toes were apparently conceited and flirtatious; they also wore the toes of their shoes out first. There had been a nice bit about ears too, pale ears belonging to a dreamer, people with small ears being tender and affectionate. If the lobes were red and strong, the owners were capable of passionate love. Shonna had just reached this part when her mother came in and she had had to stop abruptly and stuff the book under a cushion. It would not do to be caught reading such things. Elfie had looked at Peter Collins's ears. They stood out a long way from his head, like a bat's wings. According to the book that meant he was a born fighter. A man whose motto would be 'When you see a head, hit it'. That did not seem to fit Peter at all. He was a timid boy who ran away from bullies at school. The book however could not be wrong;

Peter's nature must be going to change in the years to come. Elfie wished her mother had a book like it. It held all the answers to questions you would not dare to ask a grown up. It was from here that Shonna had got the midsummer spell.

When the sixth of July turned out to be a Saturday, Elfie was nearly frantic. She did not want to miss the resurrection of the rose, but it was the day her mother always took her to the cemetery to visit her baby sister's grave. They never missed a Saturday, even though they never talked about little June at all, keeping their grief to themselves for different reasons. Mrs Brown hugged her sorrow jealously, excluding even her husband. She felt it as being personal to herself alone and took solace only in the company of other bereaved parents, scanning the obituary columns nightly and writing letters of condolence, most of which she never posted.

Elfie kept off the subject because it made her mother sad. She just wished that she could hold the baby once more and feel its fat little fingers on her neck. The smell of talcum powder made her feel quite choky. They always waited for the bus in silence, and on the long walk through the cemetery Elfie felt obliged to chatter nonsense which she hoped would occupy her mother's mind. When they reached the grave, she stood and watched as the face behind the veiling tightened as her mother tried not to cry. Then Elfie would feel a large lump rising in her throat until she could hardly swallow, and had to run to the fence and play with the nanny goat that grazed in the adjoining field until the lump went away. She wished her mother would leave her at home to play, where she was not reminded of all these sad things, but knew that if she asked it would put her mother into a mood that could last for days. Mrs Brown would shut herself up in the bedroom, speaking to no one, and Elfie would push notes under the door pleading with her to come out. But this week Shonna and the rose occupied Elfie's thoughts so much that the lump in her throat seemed much smaller, and she did not bother with the goat at all.

She fidgeted so much on the bus going back that her mother asked her if she felt sick or wanted the lavatory. Elfie sat back in her seat, abashed. She hoped nobody had heard. At last they arrived home and her mother settled in front of the garden window with her knitting. Elfie dashed off to call for Margaret, who she was sure would be just as eager as herself for another sight of the rose. Margaret's mother stuck her turbanned head round the door and spoke without removing her cigarette. They were all listening to ITMA, she said. Tommy Handley was such a scream. So run off and play with someone else like a good girl.

Elfie hopped along the pavement in the direction of Shonna's house, being careful not to tread on a crack, because that brought bad luck and broke your mother's back. She rang the doorbell and listened to it echo through the big hallway. The house sounded hollow and empty. Her heart missed a beat. Perhaps they were out. Then Mrs Creavy opened the door, and looked surprised to see her. 'Shonna's out,' she said in her soft Scottish brogue. 'Gone down to the field to play with some children.' Mrs Creavy shut the door.

Elfie thought 'I bet they're digging up the rose without waiting for me,' and darted through the gap in the hedge, and right into Shonna who was drilling a line of little children garbed in a motley assortment of battle-dress. She turned round and barred Elfie's way.

'Halt! Who goes there?'

'It's me. Elfie. You know it is.'

'What are you doing here? You're not invited.'

'But it's the sixth of July.'

'What's that got to do with it?'

Elfie stared at the children. They stared back. None of them were known to her. Where had Shonna gathered them from? They were little, the biggest one could not have been more than six years old. Two had saucepans on their heads, the handles down the back of their necks; metallic Davy Crocketts. There was a knight in woolly armour, a balaclava pulled over his mouth. The only girl wore a khaki jacket that reached to her knees, with the arms hanging empty over her wrists. Elfie did not want to mention the rose in front of them, and pulled Shonna to one side.

'What about the . . . you know . . . the . . . the . . .'

'Stop stuttering,' said Shonna. She faced Elfie, stern and unbending, playing a general now, a Field Marshal even. She must be teasing me, Elfie thought. Perhaps if I join in the game she will tell me her plans later.

'Can I play?' Elfie asked.

'I suppose so. Now you're here. Don't get in the way and don't ask stupid questions. This,' Shonna indicated the children, 'is war.'

'Are we going to fight?'

Shonna pointed to a pile of bows and arrows made from twigs and string. 'See these. We're going Uttley chasing.'

'Uttleys? What are they?'

'You mean who are they, stupid. They're evacs. They live in the High Street. We don't want them here. They've got nits and empitigo . . . and purple shaved heads.'

'Why are their heads purple?'

'Have you never heard of ringworm?' Shonna snapped.

'Yes. My mother gives me a chocolate tablet in the spring. It's called a wormcake.'

Shonna looked angry. 'Not those sort of worms, silly. Everyone has those. These are great big ones. Only Londoners have them. They're three feet long and live in their bodies and eat all their food. You can see them wriggling just under their skins. It's a horrible sight. They have to have their heads painted so people know and avoid them. It's catching see. Like lepers . . . only different.'

They marched up the High Street in single file. The children wavered a bit and had to be pushed back into line by Shonna. When they reached the back alleyway that ran parallel to the main street she gave the signal for silence, although as yet not one of them had spoken a word. They crept up the alley and hid behind some dustbins. The Uttleys lived with Mrs Tew, who ran the guest house next door to the funeral parlour. She was glad to have them as business was bad in wartime. The bulb fields had been given over to growing vegetables, and nobody took trips to see rows of cabbages and potatoes. She had been offered the land-girls, but they were cheeky and tried to sneak fellows in at night. The evacuees were less trouble, sleeping four to a bed. They did not eat as much as land-girls, either. A Lysol bath once a fortnight and everyone was happy.

While they were waiting in the alley a large funeral car swung out of the undertaker's gates. Shonna jumped up and tried to look inside it, but the curtains were drawn. The younger children started to get bored, and one of them whimpered, lisping that he wanted the lav. Shonna grabbed him by the shoulders and shook him till his teeth chattered. The saucepan fell off his head and clattered into the gutter.

'Stop that whining,' she shouted. But he carried on, bawling even louder until his little face grew puce and his nose started to drip. Shonna let go of him with one hand, drew it back and smacked him in the face with considerable force. The drips turned red.

'Oh look what you've done.' Elfie was horrified and she tried to put her arms round the little chap, dabbing at his nose with her hanky. He fought her off and ran up the street screaming, followed by the other children.

'We'd better hide,' said Elfie. 'We'll get into trouble.'

'See if I care. You hide. I'm staying right here.' Shonna looked defiant. She picked up one of the home-made bows and took up a defensive position at the entrance to the alley. Another hearse returned to the yard. Through a chink in the curtains they could see a coffin. But no purple heads had as yet shown themselves over Mrs Tew's fence. Tired of waiting, Shonna climbed the undertaker's wall, using sandbags as a step ladder. She sidled gingerly along the coping stone gripping the wall with her finger tips. When she came to the window she clung to the ledge and looked inside.

'You'll never guess what I can see,' she shouted down. Elfie did not answer. It was rude to stare into windows.

'There's bodies lying in rows. Thousands of them. Well quite a few. Long ones and short ones and . . . Wait a minute, there's a very little one. I wonder if it's a baby?'

Elfie stuck her fingers in her ears not wanting to hear any more, then turned and ran away up the alley. Dashing with her head down, not even seeing the father of the bloody-nosed boy who, with his son by the hand, was hurrying in Shonna's direction. But as he turned into the entrance she had virtually disappeared. Elfie looked around at the corner and saw Shonna's thighs encased in navy-blue utility knickers disappearing through the undertaker's window.

Elfie slept restlessly that night, her Saturday supper of bread and cheese and pickles sitting heavily in her stomach, making her dream. She was walking up the path to the field to dig up the rose, carrying her doll. Someone was with her but she could not see them, and a voice was shouting inside her head louder and louder 'Bury it with the rose . . . my rose . . . my rose . . . my rose.' She ran fast to get away from it, to leave the voice behind, but her feet stayed on the same spot and the path became longer and blacker. Then she looked down, and the doll's face splintered into little pieces. Elfie's heart missed a beat and she sat bolt upright in bed.

The rose! Of course. It was still in the field. Gosh, she thought, I completely forgot it. She scrambled out of bed, then remembered that it was too late. The sixth of July was over and the spell had been ruined. And what about the rose?

It would probably remain buried forever now, and Shonna had missed her chance. She would never get married. Perhaps Shonna had been telling lies though, like she often did. She had not bothered any more about the rose. Perhaps she had not got a lover after all. Elfie fell asleep with the moon shining right on her face, in spite of Margaret's warning.

The window panes of the dingy corner-shop were criss-crossed with strips of gummed brown paper, although it was doubtful if this would have held them together had a bomb fallen there. Through the small squares their faces peered eagerly, not hoping for sweets, because of rationing, or ice cream, for there was none. Mrs Bates used to freeze flavoured water and colour it with cochineal, pouring the mixture into paper cups and putting a lolly-stick in each. These were much favoured by the local children who saved their Saturday pennies to buy them.

Shonna was not as interested in the lollies as the other children, being pretty and bold enough to cadge chocolate and chewing gum from the American soldiers billeted in the town. She enjoyed standing on the running board of a jeep parked by her favourite, Hank, munching away whilst he stroked her fiery red curls. Once Elfie had crept up on them and caught them. Hank had his hand down the front of Shonna's school blouse. He saw Elfie and withdrew it quickly, his fresh young face flushing to the roots of his hair. 'Just feeling your friend's bumps of knowledge,' he drawled. 'We kind of like 'em young, down South.' He tweaked Elfie's plaits. Shonna stared at her insolently, daring her to say something. But even though she knew it was wrong, Elfie could think of nothing to say.

It was not lollies the girls were after today. Their noses were pressed quite flat, as they concentrated on one item in the window: a book. It was one of a dusty assortment of second-hand paperbacks that Elfie's mother called 'the penny dreadfuls', and which Elfie was forbidden to look at even through the window. Molly sat on the kerbstone keeping watch for grown-ups, and sifted dust and grit through her fingers.

The book in question had a lurid cover depicting an agonized-looking nun, arms crossed over her breast and eyes turned upwards in piety. It was entitled *The Awful Confessions of Maria Monk*, and on a brick wall behind her in giant size letters dripping with blood, WHAT I HAVE WRITTEN IS TRUE. It was priced fourpence, and was just within their means.

'If we all use our Saturday pennies we'll have just enough,' Elfie suggested.

'What about our Molly?' Margaret asked. 'She don't read. She'll be howling for her lolly.'

'Bugger your Molly.' Shonna was not going to be thwarted. 'She'll just have to go without for once won't she? What do you want to do? Stuff your faces or learn something *they* won't tell us.'

'What's in the book?' Margaret drew two hearts in the dust on one of the window panes and wrote M.G. loves J.D. She was not very interested.

'If I knew, stupid, I wouldn't be buying it would I? I think she has a baby. I want to find out how.'

Elfie felt a little shudder of excitement run through her. They were on the verge of the mystery world. That world inhabited by grown-ups, who put up invisible barriers. Children Keep Out. Grown-ups, who dropped their voices to a whisper and gave sly glances in their direction, as though children were beings from another world.

'If that's all you want to know, don't bother. I know how.

I were listening at the door when me Aunty Shirley told me mum.'

Elfie and Shonna turned towards her quickly, faces excited by the thought of what they were about to hear. Elfie put her hands over Molly's ears, but Margaret said not to bother because she would not understand anyway. Having gained their interest Margaret dropped her voice to a whisper.

'Yer stomach splits open down the middle. You know, where that red line is, and the baby pops out. She said it were awful and the bed looked like a butcher's shop. She lay there all naked and screaming.'

'You're wrong,' Shonna shouted triumphantly. 'Quite, quite wrong. Everyone knows how they get out. You can even read it in the *Chronicle* home medicine section. They don't pop out of your stomach at all. They're squeezed out of your vaginal.' She pointed out the part of anatomy concerned.

Elfie stood there looking at them both with wondering round eyes. What were they saying? Her mother had told her that she had found June under a gooseberry bush. Would she ever be able to trust her mother again? Of course Margaret and Shonna must be right, or anyway, one of them must be, and it sounded equally horrible whichever way it was. Fancy Margaret's Aunty Shirley being such a cheerful-looking person when she had had six children. Her own mother must be lying anyway, because they did not have a gooseberry bush.

'I'm not interested in that bit anyway,' said Shonna. 'We all know how they get out. It's how they get in that puzzles me. That's what we don't know. I think this book will tell us. Get your pennies out.'

'No. I'm gonna get a lolly instead.' Margaret was not enthusiastic. She thought she had a pretty good idea how they got in. Down in the Council houses at the lower end of Arcadia Road they got in pretty often. She was not going to tell Shonna though, because it sounded dirty, and if she was wrong she would never live it down.

Shonna started sulking, her pretty mouth pouting. 'Don't cough up and you won't get a read of the book.' Then persuasively. 'You'll be sorry, you'll see.'

Margaret weakened. Perhaps it might be good, after all. Nuns and priests weren't supposed to do anything like that, were they?

'What if we go in and just nick it? Next time she turns her back to get the lollies.'

'That would be stealing,' said Elfie firmly.

'Shut up you. Goody goody.' Shonna glared at her and made a threatening movement. 'It isn't stealing at all. No one could blame us for trying to get a bit of knowledge for ourselves. Even God would forgive us.' She poked Elfie in the chest. 'And you can go to your stupid confession and make jolly well sure that he does.' Turning back to Margaret, Shonna clapped her on the back. 'It's a brilliant idea. We'll get the book and the lollies too. No one loses out.'

Five minutes later they emerged triumphant, sucking lollies, with the book safely down the back of Molly's sunsuit. Only Elfie felt guilty because Mrs Bates had asked kindly about her mother, and had said was she feeling better now? And was she getting over it a bit? Elfie had shuffled uncomfortably as though the stolen book was flashing a warning red glow from Molly's behind. She hung her head, 'Yes. I think so.' Mrs Bates opened the door to let them out, remarking to her husband that the little Brown girl seemed terribly timid. Her mother's grieving must be affecting her.

They made for the field where some cows grazed in the summer, and sat down to read the book, cross-legged, in a ring. No fear of grown-ups coming in here, the smell of the cowpats would put them off. From a distance the girls would look as if they were reading *Beano* or *Dandy*. They took it in turns to read out loud. Shonna first, her voice brisk and matter of fact. She read well and skimmed the pages quickly, casting her eye down them for the bits she was sure were there. Elfie was a good reader for her age, only having to be helped with really long words, but she was slower and Shonna became impatient and snatched the book back.

'What about my turn?' Margaret demanded. 'It was my idea to pinch it. I want my read at it too.'

Shonna reluctantly handed the book over. Margaret was a poor reader, dropping her 'aitches' and leaving the endings off words, but she imbued the contents with dramatic quality, making up bits of her own when she did not understand what she was reading about. Elfie was very doubtful at times if the words coming from Margaret's mouth had ever been said by Maria. If they had it was not surprising that she had had to wear a hair shirt. Shonna must have been thinking the same, because she grabbed the book and said now they had all had a turn she would read the rest herself, otherwise it would get too dark for them to see.

Maria went through some very startling adventures before she was finally bricked up in a wall. In between the boring bits about religion and convent politics, Maria had got friendly with a priest, but the element of romance that they pined for was not there. Elfie was yawning and Molly had dropped off to sleep, her head resting on a dry cowpat.

In the middle of chapter nine, Maria produced a baby. It took just about one paragraph for her to do it. It did not get in or out, it just appeared. Created neatly and quickly in print. No screaming. No blood. Very disappointing. Shonna snapped the book shut, her mouth set in a tight line. On the way home she put it down a drain. Margaret was glad she had not wasted her Saturday penny. 'Ain't there a Christmas carol,' she remarked brightly, 'offspring of a virgin's tomb?'

'Womb,' Elfie corrected her. 'Offspring of a virgin's womb.'

'Listen to Mrs Clever Dick,' said Shonna bitterly. 'Mrs Know All. Tell us then, you being a Catholic and all that rubbish, what is a womb?'

Elfie did not know. The dictionary was another banned book. Margaret looked smug. 'I shall find out anyway soon, my mum is going to tell me everything I need to know as a woman, when my "country cousins" come.'

'I thought you said all your relatives live in Ermine Street,' said Elfie.

Shonna jumped up on the low school wall, where the railings had been removed to make ammunition, leaving behind little metallic blobs in the concrete. She put on her best lecturing voice and spoke down to them, wagging her finger. 'Don't take any notice of her,' she pointed the finger at Margaret. 'That's just the way her sort of people talk. They use different words for private things and think other people don't know what they're talking about. Like calling a lavatory "the bog". Country cousins. Pah! She means your monthly period. Menstruation. I had to be told because it happened to me early. I thought I was bleeding to death, but my mother says you get it every month till you're old and forty. She said to be careful of boys.'

'Oh,' said Elfie, trying hard to look as if she understood. Growing up was not sounding like too much fun. If she asked Shonna to explain, she would call her stupid, and a baby. She probably would not want to play with her any more. This was the very worst fate that Elfie could imagine. To be ignored by Shonna and left out of all her exciting games. Racking her brain for a grown-up remark, Elfie said, 'That's okay then cos I'm always careful of boys.' Margaret and Shonna went off into hoots of laughter and pushed her into her gateway, running off up the road, laughing and dragging Molly along with them.

Behind the front window curtains Elfie could see her mother fretting because she was a bit late. She did not like Shonna and wished Elfie would find a more suitable friend, some quiet little girl who would play with dolls and not climb trees, or annoy the neighbours. Mrs Brown lived in fear of the neighbours and what they thought. Elfie wondered why, as they did not really know any of them, and had never been in a neighbour's house. Everyone in the middle of Arcadia Road kept themselves to themselves. When a hole had been cut through the Browns's cellar and that of the neighbouring house, to provide an escape route should a bomb fall, Mr Brown had attempted a bit of camaraderie, shouting through the hole to old Mr Hornsby, 'Watch out for your valuables now.' The next day the hole had been filled in. Now Mrs Brown hurried to the door exclaiming, 'Where on earth have you been. It's almost dusk.'

Elfie settled herself at the scrubbed kitchen table, looking at the verdigris growing on the pipes above the copper in the corner, where her mother boiled the clothes every Monday, thinking what to say. Her mother put a pan of milk on the stove and started spreading some bread and marge with Marmite. 'Have you been with that Shonna?' she asked.

'Yes,' said Elfie. There was no point in lying. Her mother must have seen them from the window. 'We've been to the field to look at the cows.'

Mrs Brown's face hardened. 'What for?' If Shonna was looking at cows there must be something behind it. She was not known in the area as an animal lover, and had once been seen kicking the Hornsbys's old cat. 'Were they all cows?' Mrs Brown asked doubtfully, hoping Elfie had not seen any-thing she should not have seen. You never knew with animals; they were so primitive. Shonna would be just the one to look at something nasty like that. Even though she lived in the biggest and smartest house in Arcadia Road, you could not make a silk purse out of a sow's ear. There were rumours that her mother had once been in service and had run off with the son of the house. How disgraceful. It must be true because she did all her work in a pinny, and could be seen scrubbing and polishing any day.

Mrs Brown had a daily woman for the rough work, even

though some of the carpets were going bald and the linoleum was worn to the canvas in places. Elfie liked the daily, Mrs Baggett, who had a little boy called Tyrone, and who let her help with the dusting. She called Elfie 'my little princess'. Mrs Brown occupied her spare time in ladylike pursuits such as turning shirt collars and doing invisible darns on sheets. She made most of Elfie's clothes too. Neatly stitched and never looking quite like shop-bought dresses. Now Mrs Brown went into her familiar routine of 'Why don't you find a little friend more like yourself.'

Elfie closed her ears and ate her bread and Marmite. Her mother just liked moaning and did not expect an answer anyway. Elfie kissed her goodnight and went up to bed, to the little room at the front of the house that she shared with her teddy bear and a baby doll. Its eyes, that once snapped open and shut, were fixed and staring where they had been mended with glue, but it had lovely hand-embroidered clothes, handed down by Elfie's Grandma, and once worn by a real baby.

She snuggled down into the lumpy feather mattress and smoothed her hands over the quilted satin eiderdown, loving its silky feel. She thought of Maria Monk lying in her little cell on the hard wooden pallet, and wondered if the nuns at the Convent she attended with Shonna slept on pallets too. She did not think so, neither did she think that they whipped themselves, even though they did slap little girls. The thought of Sister Ignatious's skinny legs sticking out from beneath a hair shirt was enough to make you hysterical. She certainly was not built for leaning romantically against Convent walls. Her eyes glinted, cold and efficient, from behind steel-framed glasses. They were not the sort of eyes to turn softly upwards in supplication. And nobody, not even Father Dominic, who was fat and downright ugly with his red skin and little piggy nose, would be attracted by her wrinkled walnut face. What about Sister Julie Anne? She had been pretty. Elfie tried to banish the painful memories that tumbled into her mind.

There was the quiet corner of the Convent garden where they were forbidden to play. Shonna had taken her there one day to peep through the wooden railings to where a statue of the Holy Virgin looked down on a few sad home-made crosses and jam jars filled with wild flowers that stood lopsidedly among the grasses and weeds. They had stood there, noses dappled with sunshine. Gosh, that was a year ago now.

'It doesn't look like a graveyard to me. Our little June's got an angel on her grave and a cross, and a big white vase with lots of flowers.'

'That,' Shonna had said, 'is because your little June died in a state of grace. Babies do unless they're not baptized. This place is for the nuns who didn't. The wicked ones. It's unhallowed gound.' Elfie shivered and crossed herself quickly.

'You're fibbing! Everyone knows you tell tales, Shonna Creavy. There aren't any bad nuns. They all go straight to heaven when they die. It's their vacation. My mother says so.'

'That's only because your sainted mother is a Catholic, who believes everything the priest tells her. Can't think for herself. Quick, here comes Sister Ignatious. We'll get detention if we're caught here.'

Elfie rolled on to her side and tried counting sheep. As the sheep jumped over the fence their faces looked like Sister Julie Anne, and their black ears like wimples. Sister Julie Anne had taught Elfie the piano, her mother saying that all well brought up girls should be able to play something at a party, if asked. But Elfie was not musical and had no sense of rhythm, and Sister Julie used to rap her on the knuckles with a ruler. Elfie could not wait for the lessons to end, when she could jump up from the music stool to bid Sister a hasty 'Good afternoon'. One day her undignified exit was halted by Sister asking if she would deliver a letter for her on the way home. Elfie gladly complied. Anything to get in Sister Julie Anne's good books, and it was not even out of her way.

The note was addressed to Miss Brennan, the games

mistress. It was the first of many, and soon Sister Julie Anne stopped rapping Elfie on the knuckles, which was nice. Miss Brennan was sporty and leapt about the netball field in shorts, her hair cropped in bangs, American fashion. She was idolized by all the girls, especially Shonna, who went out of her way to be noticed, cartwheeling all over the place in a manner most unbecoming to a Convent girl. Elfie jealously guarded the secret of the notes. Had not Sister told her not to tell anyone? Nuns did not have money for stamps anyway. The notes were a bond between the three of them. A small piece of life she did not want to share with Shonna. Elfie felt as though it set her a bit apart from the other girls, even if Miss Brennan did single her out on the hockey field, and make fun of her because she could not run very fast. Shonna's sharp eyes missed nothing and one day she whispered to her at afternoon prayers, 'I don't think Miss Brennan likes you. I've noticed how she shouts. I expect it's because you're fat and clumsy.'

'I'm not then. And she does like me.'

'Prove it,' said Shonna spitefully.

'I can then. I go to Miss Brennan's house. She gives me cake and lemonade.'

'I don't believe you. Liar,' Shonna whispered.

'It's true then.' Elfie drew the latest note from the safety of her knicker pocket and passed it over to Shonna. 'See! I take notes to her from Sister Julie Anne. Don't tell anyone. It's a secret.'

Sister Ignatious, high up on the rostrum, saw the note change hands. Was this another of those rude poems that were circulating with alarming regularity? The war was causing a decline in moral standards, she was sure. Boys had been seen lately lurking on the edge of the playing field, ogling girls who had shortened their gym tunics to a most indecent length. She would see about that tomorrow. Meanwhile Sister Ignatious girded up her habit and strode the length of the hall, yanking Shonna and Elfie out of the line by their collars.

'Do you not know then, you girls, how rude it is to whisper?

Especially at holy moments like Assembly. It's an insult to the Lord Jesus Christ himself. Now, shame the devil and tell the words out loud.'

Shonna looked humble. She folded her hands in front of her and hung her head. 'Sorry Sister,' she said politely. 'Elfreda was only telling me how much she admires Miss Brennan.'

'Indeed. Well that is a nice thing for us to know. Tell us more, Elfreda.'

'No.' Elfie dropped her eyes. 'There's nothing to tell. Nothing.' she repeated loudly.

'Elfie goes to Miss Brennan's house, Sister,' Shonna volunteered. 'Miss Brennan gives her lemonade and cakes, for bringing notes from Sister Julie Anne.' She paused and looked sweetly up to Sister Ignatious, ignoring Elfie's pleading glances. 'Isn't Miss Brennan kind, Sister?'

'Indeed she is.' Sister's face betrayed no emotion. Elfie's soul felt sharp daggers from Sister's eyes piercing it. Sister reached out and took the note from Shonna in a hand withered like a claw and tucked it straight into the capacious pocket of her black habit. Rows of girls' faces swam in front of Elfie's eyes, laughing faces, smirking faces. Glad I'm not you faces. Elfie would catch it now.

Sister went back to the platform and carried on with prayers. 'In the name of the Father,' she intoned, whilst Elfie felt a surge of hatred for Shonna.

'Tell tale tit!' Elfie's voice rang out above the girlish hum.

'And of the Son.' Sister's voice rose higher.

'Your tongue shall be split,' Elfie shouted, her round face scarlet with temper.

'AndoftheHolyGhostAmenClassdismissed.' Sister did not even stop to draw a breath. She was beside Elfie in two strides, and pulled her outside the door by her arm and gave her a lecture on manners. She exhorted her to say three 'Hail Marys' and an 'Our Father'.

'May God forgive you because you have an evil temper.'

They had returned from school after the summer break and there was a new games mistress, soft and fluffy, with a long divided skirt, instead of shorts. Shonna did not do any more cartwheels. Elfie's music lessons had suddenly been stopped. On account, said her mother, of her having no ear for it. Elocution lessons had been substituted, and Elfie gradually forgot the incident of the note and played once more with Shonna in the Convent gardens. One day as the leaves were starting to fall, Shonna took her by the arm and steered her away from the other girls towards the forbidden corner. Shonna pointed through the railings to a new cross. 'Who do you think that's for?' she asked.

'I don't know,' said Elfie, puzzled.

'It's for your favourite. Sister Julie Anne. She's dead, you know.'

'She's not,' said Elfie, as a sudden gust of autumn wind swirled the fallen leaves into a heap on the new grave, and the chill in the air marked the end of those summer days.

'She is then. Killed herself for love of Miss Brennan. I blame you.'

Elfie burst into tears. Shonna was being cruel. It could not be true. Nuns loved only Jesus. They were brides of God. Her mother said so. She said also that one day Elfie might be one too. Shonna was talking nonsense to upset her, because she was still jealous. How could Sister Julie Anne love Miss Brennan, who was not a man? If she had killed herself she would not go to heaven. And if she had not killed herself, why was she in the unhallowed ground? Elfie ran away, shouting, 'You're lying . . . lying . . . lying!'

Shonna cupped her hands to her mouth and called after her, 'Dying . . . dying . . . dying'. Her mocking voice chased Elfie into sleep that night.

3

The summer holidays were dragging on a bit. Nobody could go to the seaside because of the barbed wire and the landmines and all. Shonna was fed up. She struck out the 'A' from Baring-in-the-Marshes and substituted an 'O'. Boring-in-the-Marshes is what it should be called, she said, and tried out the worst curse she could dream up on Hitler. 'Damn his eyes and may his blood turn to piss!'

'Curses like chickens come home to roost,' said Elfie. But Shonna just turned the signpost round the wrong way, so that people heading for Norwich would end up at Baring. That would fix them.

'You ain't got no power over Hitler,' said Margaret. 'He's much wickeder than you.'

They sat beneath the signpost at the edge of the town, listlessly playing jacks with some pebbles they had found in the park. Suddenly Shonna jumped up scattering the stones on the ground. 'I wish something exciting would happen like a bomb or a blitz. Just to liven things up a bit, I mean.'

'Then you might be dead,' said Margaret, 'and you wouldn't be around to see it.'

'Don't worry, it'll never happen. This place isn't even worth bombing. Hitler wouldn't waste one on it.'

Elfie said, 'Think up a new game. Please Shonna. Think up something exciting.'

Shonna brightened. 'I know. We'll have a party.'

'We can't,' pointed out Elfie. 'There's the rationing.'

'Doesn't bother me. My dad can get black market,' Shonna bragged.

'He'll go to clink.' Margaret picked up the jacks and put them in her pocket. They would do for a swapsie later. 'What kind of a party will it be?' she asked. 'I'm not going to one of them where you play oranges and lemons and pass the parcel. So there!'

'Nobody asked you to,' returned Shonna smartly. 'I'm having a Hallowe'en party, see.'

'Well, it ain't Hallowe'en until October.' Margaret set off to walk back to town.

'There's no law against having a party for it, is there?' Shonna pulled Elfie to her feet and went after Margaret. Elfie jumped up and down shouting, 'Hallowe'en is witches and spells. Hallowe'en is witches and . . .'

'Be quiet you!' Shonna glared at her.

'But can we peel apples and throw the skins over our shoulders to see our lover's name?' Elfie hopped up and down on the grass verge trying to keep pace with the older girls.

'That's kid's stuff. No, we're going to do grown-up things. We'll have fruit punch and baked potatoes and . . . we'll play Ouija.'

'Is that like postman's knock?' said Margaret. 'Will there be boys coming?'

'No, there'll be ghosts.'

Margaret's face fell. Two letters and a parcel from a ghost were not what she had in mind. 'What's this Ouija then?'

'It's a grown-up's game,' Shonna explained. 'They play it when children are in bed. They call up the spirits and ask them questions. It's a big round board with a "yes" at the top and a "no" at the bottom. That's why it's called Ouija, see.'

They looked at her, puzzled. Shonna carried on, 'From the French and the German for yes. Oui? Ja? Get it?'

'Ja,' said Margaret. 'But where will we get it from?'

'I've got one. Found it under my mother's bed. She keeps her fortune-telling cards there too. People come to hear their futures. Most of them go away crying.' They reached Margaret's house and sat down on the wall.

'Is your mother a gypsy?' Elfie asked. 'My mother's only got a chamber pot under her bed. But it is a nice one . . . with roses on it.'

'Your mother . . .' said Shonna, giving her a look of contempt. 'Peeing in a pot. Too lazy to go to the bathroom.'

'We have pots too. Our facilities is outside, see,' said Margaret.

'But is your mother a gypsy?' Elfie persisted.

'I've told you a thousand times,' said Shonna, 'she's got second sight. It's not the same thing. Gypsies are common. She can read the tarot cards and that's very clever. So there.'

She pushed Elfie backwards off the wall causing her to land heavily in a bed of nettles, the only sign of vegetation in Margaret's garden. Elfie squealed and jumped about, spat on her hand and rubbed the raised blotches. Margaret started searching for a dock leaf to put on the stings. Shonna watched them for a bit, laughing, then spat on the wall and blew gently on the globule till it hardened. It took a long time, but she had nothing else to do. At last she rubbed her finger over the surface of the little mound she had created and purred, 'There. That'll last forever. It's my very own mark. Made from my very own body.' She paused and looked round to make sure they were listening, and then said very slowly, emphasizing every word, 'Even after I'm dead and gone.'

'And that'll be sooner than you think if me mum catches you a-spitting on our wall. You wouldn't like it if someone spit on your'n.' Margaret was offended. She pulled Molly inside the house and slammed the door.

'You've upset her,' said Elfie.

'I don't care. It's only an old Council house. What's she making such a fuss about? People spit on the walls all the time in them.' Shonna marched off in a temper, and Elfie ran after her to make the peace in case she called the exciting party off.

When the day arrived Elfie pleaded with her mother for something new to wear, but Mrs Brown said there were no coupons for that sort of thing. They all had to be saved for Father's suits. It was more important that he should go to work looking decent, and it didn't matter much about Elfie, as who was going to look at her, anyway? He was the bread-winner, wasn't he?

Elfie got her white organdie dress out of the wardrobe and laid it out on the bed, like a body. The blue ribbon sash draped around it pinched the waist in to a size that bore no resemblance to her plump middle. The buttons hardly fastened at the back now. I wonder why I get fatter in spite of the rationing, she thought. Most of the girls from school had best dresses made from parachute silk. That was really smart. Perhaps one day an airman would be shot down over their garden and she would bandage up his wounds and he would give her his parachute. She would have it made into a dress with bishop sleeves and a tie belt and pleats all round the skirt. He could have the white organdie in exchange, and give it to his daughter.

Her mother was heating the curling tongs in the fire, and started to crimp Elfie's hair, winding it round and round to make it curl. Trying to fashion ringlets, Mrs Brown pulled it up so hard that Elfie's cheek went with it and her face became lopsided. 'Ouch!' she squeaked. The kitchen was full of the smell of burnt wool. Perhaps it's just as well there aren't so many parties, she thought, or I could be frizzed bald by the time I'm ten.

Mrs Brown stepped back to admire the effect of curls on her daughter, and sighed. Shirley Temple was such a pretty child. Was it the dimples that made such a difference? She pressed a small box of chocolates into Elfie's hand. 'Here take these. You can't go empty handed.'

Elfie set off happily to call for Margaret. Mrs Brown did not approve of her as a friend either. The Groutages dropped their 'aitches' and went bare-legged, even in winter. A sure sign of poor-quality people. Mrs Groutage kept Elfie waiting on the doorstep; she never asked anyone in. It was six o'clock and she still had her curlers in. Was she going to bed early or were they still there from the morning? How could anyone sleep with all that ironmongery in their heads? Elfie peeped in the front window through a rent in the curtains. The tiny room that Margaret always referred to as 'our parlour' was empty, except for a bicycle belonging to Margaret's brother Tom. Margaret said they only used the room at Christmas. Wherever did they all sit?

Suddenly from above came shouting and swearing that would have shamed even Shonna. Eventually Margaret came out with Molly, her eyes red. Neither of them wore party frocks and they carried no gifts. Elfie felt sorry for them. 'You can hold my present if you like,' she said.

'It ain't that. I don't care if I've got no present. I wouldn't give her one anyway. No. It's Mum.' She shook her fist in the direction of the house. As she turned her head, Elfie could see the weals made by Mrs Groutage's fingers.

'What did she slap you for?'

'I were looking under her bed. Thought I might find summit, like Shonna. To take to the party. There was balloons there. Funny long white ones. I were blowing one up for our Molly when she came in. Dead mean she is. She took it off me and give me a slap round the chops. What's she want with balloons anyway? She's not a kid.'

'Perhaps she's saving them for Christmas,' said Elfie. 'Or perhaps she's going to have a party of her own.'

★

Shonna's house was a large villa set back from the road, with impressive black and white gables. They crunched up the long gravel drive, swinging Molly between them. Margaret looked happier as she started to forget her troubles. As they reached the front porch, Mr Creavy came out. He tipped his hat to them.

'Are you going fire-watching?' Margaret asked him. 'Yes,' he answered shortly and carried on down the drive. Elfie felt that he did not like children.

'You've forgotten your helmet,' Margaret called after him. But he did not come back for it.

Elfie lifted Molly up to ring the bell. She kept her finger on it for a long time, dribbling happily. Shonna came to the door, wearing a long black skirt that had once been her mother's. Silver paper stars and moons were sewn on to it and Shonna's red curls were enveloped in a filmy pink scarf, tied gypsy fashion. Long hoop earrings dangled from her lobes. The whole effect was somewhat spoiled by the school blouse she had on. She knew they were impressed and danced up the passage ahead of them. 'Coo, don't she look grand,' Margaret whispered to Elfie. 'Like *Madonna of the Seven Moons*. When I grow up I'll wear clothes like that all the time and have lovers like Stewart Granger. We'll read each other's palms all night.' To Shonna she said, 'You look a right sight. What you done to yourself?'

Shonna took them into the lounge, where she had drawn the curtains to make it darker. The room was lit with turnip lanterns. Evil faces glowed from the picture rail. Molly did not like it; she clung to Margaret and started to cry. Shonna raised a hand to hit her, but her mother came in with a plate of fairy cakes, so she pretended to be adjusting the scarf, and waited till Mrs Creavy had gone, then stuffed a whole fairy cake into the child's mouth to shut her up.

Elfie looked at the tea-table, spread with a crisp white damask cloth, and china plates that all matched. Sparkling

crystal glasses surrounded a jug of orange with real pieces of
fruit floating in it. The centre piece was a large green jelly
rabbit with eyes made from glacé cherries. He quivered on a
bed of pink blancmange. Elfie thought she had never seen
anything so pretty. It would be a shame to eat him. She stood
staring at him while Shonna fished the Ouija board out from
under the sofa cushions.

'Quick,' Shonna said. 'While she's out getting the tea ready.'

'She's the cat's aunt,' Margaret told her.

Shonna pushed her out of the way and plonked the board
on the coffee table. Then she took a glass and up-ended it on
the board.

'That's it. We can start. Each of you put a finger on it and
think hard. The glass will move by itself. It's the spirit that
does it. Don't force it. If you do you're cheating. It's on your
mother's life.'

Molly put her pudgy little fingers on the glass and twirled
it round. Shonna tapped her warningly on the head. 'The
spirit may move through the afflicted,' she said. 'They sometimes speak in tongues.'

Margaret jumped up angrily. 'Afflicted yourself. She ain't
afflicted. She's just a bit slow, that's all.'

Elfie intervened. 'It does say in the Bible that it's a sin to
communicate with spirits.'

'It says in the Bible that the Angel Gabriel visited the Virgin
Mary. I suppose he wasn't a spirit. So what's good enough for
her is good enough for you. Let's get on with it. If you don't
want to play you can go home.'

Molly had lost interest and wandered to the tea-table, and
gently poked her finger into the rabbit. The jelly resisted it.
The three girls knelt down at the table and put their fingers
on the glass. Shonna called out in a hollow voice, 'Is there
anyone there?' The glass moved slowly round the board to
Yes. Elfie shivered excitedly.

'Quick! Quick! Someone's there. Ask it something.'

'Is my mother in the kitchen?' said Shonna. The glass stayed on Yes.

'There you are. The spirit knows.'

'Who are you?' Elfie asked it. The glass started moving slowly in a clockwise direction, spelling out the letters JUNE . . . Shonna nudged Elfie. 'There you are. It's your baby.'

'Don't be silly,' said Elfie. 'She was only nine months old. She couldn't talk you know.'

'Anything is possible to the spirits,' said Shonna.

'I'll ask it summit,' Margaret giggled, blushing a bit. 'Does Jimmy Day love me?'

The glass positively whizzed down to No. Margaret jabbed Shonna in the chest, across the table. 'Hey! You pushed that. I seen you. You're cheating at your own party.'

'No I'm not then. This spirit is obviously talking about love, the proper sort. True heartfelt love. Not going down the air raid shelter with boys. See.'

Elfie saw a chance to get a question in while they were arguing. 'Will I pass my scholarship?' There was no reply. Shonna and Margaret were still glaring at each other across the table. Elfie repeated the question.

'Don't be boring,' said Shonna. 'It'll get fed up and go away. Let's ask it what's going to happen to us when we grow up?'

'I know what's going to happen to me,' Margaret boasted. 'I'm going to marry Stewart Granger.'

Shonna laughed, and pressed their fingers to the glass again. 'Tell us, O spirit, what is the future for Margaret?' The glass moved round the board at a brisk pace, spelling out FACTORY.

'Well it's got that wrong. I'm going to be a film star. I'm going to be like Greer Garson. So there.'

'The spirit is never wrong,' Shonna replied smugly. 'I'll ask it mine.'

Molly had edged back into the group now, tired of the

rabbit. Elfie took hold of her hand and placed a finger gently with theirs on the glass. Shonna was commanding the spirit, 'Tell me my future.'

This time there was a very long pause, as though the glass was struggling which way to go. Perhaps, thought Elfie, the Spirit is thinking. Then it suddenly shot round the board backwards spelling out the letters SHONNABLOODDIE. They all turned to stare at her, and she leapt up dragging Molly from the table.

'I knew it,' Shonna shouted. 'She's a jinx! She's a Jonah! She's a witch! She's put a curse on me.'

'No she ain't,' Margaret retorted. 'She can't even write. It's the spirit moving through her. You said so yourself. You said the spirit can't lie.'

'Anyway,' said Elfie, 'if you die there may not be blood. You could have a pillow put over your face, like the little Princes in the tower.'

'Thank you,' said Shonna bitterly, and stuffed the Ouija board back under the cushion. Then she went and sat in the armchair in the corner and glowered at them. They felt very uncomfortable and stood around shuffling their feet, not knowing what to do.

Elfie whispered to Margaret, 'Go on. Own up. It'll be all right then.'

'Sorry Shonna,' Margaret muttered.

Shonna took no notice and went on scowling at them, her arms folded across her chest. Mrs Creavy came back in with a plate of bread and butter. She seemed to sense an atmosphere and said nervously, 'Shonna dear, would you like to hand this round to your guests?'

'No,' said Shonna, and turned her face to the wall.

'Come on dear, this is no way to treat your friends,' said her mother. Shonna got up and walked across to the tea-table. She picked up the heavy silver serving spoon and held it threateningly over the rabbit's back.

'Not the jelly dear,' said her mother. 'Bread and butter first.'

Shonna lifted her arm and brought the spoon down smack on the rabbit's back. It quivered slightly but remained intact. Elfie breathed a sigh of relief. She did not want the rabbit broken, not even to eat it. Shonna moved forward quickly and tugged at the tablecloth, up-ending everything on to the floor. Now the rabbit lay, a shapeless splodge of green jelly amid the broken biscuits and china on the hearth. Mrs Creavy went very pale. Still holding the plate she caught hold of Shonna and said: 'You naughty girl! Now apologize.'

Shonna shook herself free from her mother's hand. 'No,' she said defiantly. Mrs Creavy now looked decidedly flustered. She turned to Elfie. 'Have a bit of bread and butter, dear.' Elfie politely took a piece and put it in her mouth. Encouraged, Mrs Creavy offered the plate to Margaret as though bread and butter was the panacea for all quarrels, but Margaret tossed her head.

'I think we'll be getting off home if it's all the same to you, Missus. Your Shonna don't seem very well.' She looked across at Shonna and added spitefully, 'Perhaps she ought to go to bed without her tea.'

Mrs Creavy made no effort to detain them and stood looking at Shonna as though mesmerized, still clutching the plate of bread and butter. They gathered up their coats in silence and made for the door. Molly bent down and tried to pick up a piece of rabbit but it slipped through her fingers. She howled with disappointment as they pulled her away. Elfie felt like howling too. As soon as they got outside she turned on Margaret.

'Why did you do it? You spoiled the party.'

'I didn't,' said Margaret.

'Yes you did. You owned up.'

'Only because you told me to. Look, you don't think I'd have done it do you before we had tea. Knowing her temper.'

'Then who did it?' Elfie felt a cold little shiver down her back. She wouldn't play Ouija again. Never. You didn't get scared with snakes and ladders or ludo.

She looked at Margaret, but her mouth was shut tight in a thin line. You could not tell what she was thinking, but further down the road she said, 'Anyway, it weren't much of a party. When I have one I'm going to have kissing games and lots of boys.' She pushed Elfie in at the gate and did not even say goodbye. I've fallen out with both of them now, Elfie thought sadly, I just can't seem to get it right. She had not expected Margaret to own up, anyway.

Elfie's mother was surprised to see her home so early and said it must have been a very short party. She felt some people she could name only gave parties to get the presents. Elfie did not tell her about the Ouija game, or the tantrum. She just said that Shonna had been sick and they had thought it polite to leave early.

'Sick?' said Mrs Brown. 'I suppose she guzzled all those chocolates I sent her. How greedy! Well, it's us that will have to go without. That was a whole month's sweet ration.'

4

The note was on bright yellow paper, written in purple ink, and addressed in Shonna's distinctive forward-sloping hand. Decorated with little violets it was sealed with the letters H.O.L.L.A.N.D. This must be a new version of S.W.A.L.K. which everyone knew meant 'sealed with a loving kiss'. Good job she had found it before her mother got up. She opened everyone's letters, even Daddy's. Elfie took it up to the bedroom.

Make some excuse not to go to school with your father tomorrow. There's something important we've got to do. Don't tell Margaret. Yours forever. S.C.

The weekly drive to school with her father was one of the highlights of the week. He was the only man in Arcadia Road to have a car, as he had a petrol ration for his government job which took him away from home for most of the week. Mr Brown was too old to join the forces, but had fought in World War One and been gassed. Elfie was proud of this and pointed out the marks on his face where the mustard gas had eaten in. Shonna said, 'Pooh! It's not true. He's had the pox.' Her father was not in the forces either, but Shonna said he had been invalided out, surrounding him with an aura of glamour. Margaret insisted it was because he was batty. She had been told he behaved funny when there was a full moon. She said as much to Shonna, hinting that when the moon was up he growled and his hair grew long. But Shonna said, 'Don't be daft. All he does is shift the furniture around a bit.'

The car was black and very shiny; the girls all helped to polish it on a Sunday morning. The upholstery was real leather and smelled like new shoes when Elfie put her nose up against it. Mr Brown finished work on Thursday night, and on Friday morning he would drive the girls to school as a treat. On the way they often passed Mr Creavy riding his bicycle to work. When it rained he covered his dark suit with a set of shiny yellow oilskins like a fisherman. Margaret always pointed him out, but Shonna would pretend she could not see him.

This week Elfie told her father that she had been asked to visit a sick teacher with Shonna, and there would only be Margaret going in the car. Mr Brown raised his eyebrows wondering that if this was the case, whether he should be asked to go at all. But as it was raining hard and he had noticed Margaret's poor shoes, he shrugged and said, 'All right dear, but take an umbrella if you're walking.' Her mother asked if it was wise to call on teachers if they were not well. There was scarlet fever about. Elfie said they would not go in, but just stand at the door, and enquire.

'It might be polite to take some flowers.' Mrs Brown took a coin from her purse.

Elfie bought a bunch of chrysanthemums. She would give them to one of the nuns for the chapel, she thought. Shonna asked her about the flowers, and said it was a stupid thing to do, to buy them. Elfie should have kept the shilling, for the pictures.

'Where are we going?' Elfie asked her.

'We're going to school,' said Shonna. 'But we're going by bus. I've got the fares.'

'It's only two stops, and I have the umbrella. We could walk.' Elfie was very disappointed. School was not an adventure.

'We could, but we're not going to because I want to go on the bus to get a good look at the conductress.'

'Why? Do you want to be one when you grow up? I don't. My mother says it's only a wartime job. They wear trousers and whistle. It's only suitable to certain types of women.'

'Your snobby mother may be right for once,' Shonna rejoined. 'This one is an adulteress.'

Elfie stopped. 'An adulteress! That's in the Bible, isn't it? It says you mustn't do it. What is it?'

'It's a sin. A mortal sin. One of the seven deadly ones. It means taking a lover when you're married already. And it's against the commandments too.'

By now they had reached the bus shelter and dived inside, the flowers dripping pools of water on to the floor, and into Elfie's socks. The rain from the brims of their velour hats dripped steadily down their necks. They watched Mr Brown drive by, Margaret sitting warm and snug beside him in Elfie's seat. He peered out of the windscreen, the wipers flashing in front of his eyes, without seeing the girls. Soon afterwards Mr Creavy cycled by in oilskins, head bent against the weather. He did not see them either. Elfie took off her hat and shook her head like a spaniel emerging from a lake. The bus was late, and they clambered on board. Shonna jostled Elfie for the seat nearest the aisle, to get a better view of the adulteress.

The conductress swung towards them, her young body clad in navy slacks and a jacket embellished with epaulettes and silver buttons. She had hair as red as Shonna's, only straight and swept up at the sides with two grips in the latest fashion. She was chewing gum, her jaw moving rhythmically, one cheek bulging. She said 'Fares please' out of the corner of her vermilion mouth.

Shonna looked her up and down insolently. 'Two fourpenny ones.'

'I'll give you a fourpenny one!' The clippie grinned and chucked Elfie under the chin. 'Cheer up, big eyes,' she said. She looked very young under the pancake make-up and crimson lipstick. She gave them the tickets and walked away to ring the bell, hips swinging with the motion of the bus. They watched every movement she made. When they alighted at the town centre, Elfie remarked, 'She's very pretty and she doesn't look wicked to me. Perhaps she doesn't read the Bible and doesn't know about adultery. Margaret's mother has lovers. Lots of them. Margaret told me. And her dad's away fighting at the front. Perhaps it's allowed in wartime. Maybe it's not as bad as we think.'

'You'd think it was bad if it was your father she was adulterating with, wouldn't you?' Shonna shouted.

'Your father!' exclaimed Elfie, as a picture of Mr Creavy complete with oilskins cycled through her mind. Was he the stuff that sinners were made from?

'Yes. My father. I've seen them together. He meets her off the bus when he's supposed to be fire-watching. They go away arm in arm. If that isn't adultery I don't know what is.'

She put her head on her arms up against the wall and started to sob. Sobs that shook her whole body. Elfie stood looking on helplessly, not knowing what to say to comfort her, the soggy flowers trailing on the ground.

'Can't you tell your mother?' she said at last.

Shonna turned round sharply. Her eyes were quite dry. 'She's got nothing to do with it,' she said. They walked to the Convent in silence and tried to sneak in quietly.

'You girls have missed Assembly.' Sister Ignatious was lurking by the cloakrooms, waiting for late-comers. Shonna snatched the dripping flowers from Elfie's hand, held them out, and said with a sweet smile, 'I had to queue for them, Sister.'

Sister Ignatious took hold of the sorry bouquet, saying, 'It is the thought that counts, I suppose. Thank you Shonna.' She turned to Elfie. 'You can take a detention.'

On the way home Shonna said to Elfie, 'Look, I've got an idea. I know how to get rid of her, that adulteress. Get her away from my father.'

'How?' said Elfie, cross about the hundred lines she was going to have to write tonight. She would have to miss *Children's Hour*.

'I'll write him a letter and pretend it's from her. Calling the whole thing off. Finishing it.'

'What will you say? You don't even know her name, do you?'

'That doesn't matter. I'll copy something out of the *Chronicle*. There's a whole chapter on letter writing. There's bound to be a suitable bit. I'll do it tonight.'

Elfie thought that she did not blame Mr Creavy for preferring the bus conductress. Mrs Creavy was a creepy sort of person, and that second sight must be a difficult thing to live with. Mr Creavy was very handsome in a frightening sort of way. She wished her own father was tall and dark instead of being tubby and grey.

The next day Shonna showed Elfie the letter. It was most impressive and had been typed on her father's machine with one finger.

'I found just the thing. It's called "Rejecting the attentions of an unwelcome suitor". It only needed a few alterations.' Shonna cleared her throat and started to read:

'Dear Sir,
      It has recently been very obvious, not only to myself, but to my friends, that you have gone out of your way to meet me as I travel on the bus where I'm employed. I am writing to say, briefly but firmly, that these attentions are distasteful to me. I should have thought that your own common sense

would have told you that at no time have I offered you the slightest encouragement, and I want you to accept this letter as an actual request that you should leave me to my own devices in future.

Yours faithfully,

Bus conductress. (Route Five).

'There! What do you think to that?'

Elfie looked at her admiringly. 'It's very good. The *Chronicle* always gets things right, doesn't it?'

'Yes,' said Shonna. 'It's polite but firm. It should edge him off once and for all. I shall buy a stamp and send it through the post. Then I'll follow him on Friday night and see what happens.'

'Can I come with you?' Elfie asked eagerly.

'No. Better not. You're a bit clumsy for tracking and I don't want to be seen. Watch at the window on Saturday morning and I'll pass by and give you a sign.'

After they returned from the cemetery, Elfie, positioned herself at the window and waited anxiously all afternoon for Shonna, but she never appeared. Next week, when Elfie asked her at school what had happened and had the letter worked, she said of course it had. Everything she did worked OK, Elfie should know that by now. But Elfie said, 'What about the sign? Did you forget?' After all, she had wasted a whole afternoon watching out of the window. Shonna looked puzzled, and said, 'What sign? I don't know what you're talking about.'

They rode on the bus once more, this time in high spirits to see the clippie again. Would she look different? Sad and broken-hearted? She took the fares this time without joking. Shonna whispered, 'You can see she's suffering, can't you?' Elfie felt sorry for her. She seemed to be clicking the ticket machine much harder than before, and although Shonna kept looking round trying to engage her attention, she stared determinedly out of the back window whistling 'White Cliffs of Dover'. They jumped off at the town hall and Shonna grabbed Elfie by the arm, drawing her attention to a poster pasted on the wall, right next to the one telling them that careless talk cost lives.

'Look at that. There's a concert party coming. Forces' Favourites. Do you think your stuffy old parents will let you go?'

'No, I shouldn't think so,' said Elfie. 'We're still in mourning you see. We don't go out anywhere.'

'Don't be silly. You can't be still in mourning. It was two years ago. They just tell you that because they're mean. Don't want to pay for anything. Take the money out of your piggy bank.'

'There's nothing in it except at Christmas and birthdays.'

'I'll ask Margaret then.' Shonna did not want to go by herself; it wasn't such fun. They knocked at Margaret's door and told her about the concert. Mrs Groutage had her feet up, listening to the radio. She called from the kitchen, 'Concert party, eh? Who's in it? Anyone we know?'

'A lot of handsome young men, singing and dancing and telling jokes. They're the forces' favourites,' replied Shonna. Margaret said tartly, 'If they're so young and handsome why aren't they in the army?'

'Wounded out,' said Shonna.

'And dancing about on their crutches,' laughed Mrs Groutage. 'If we've got any money come Friday, we'll go.'

Shonna turned away in disgust. Those Groutages never had any money, Friday or any other day. She took the girls back to the town hall and they all looked at the poster again. 'See what you'll be missing,' she told them.

'There's a talent contest for local children on the Friday too,' said Elfie mournfully. 'I would like to recite my piece.'

'And so you shall,' Shonna declared. 'You and Margaret

can go in for the contest and you'll get free tickets. I'll pay and sit in a seat and watch you. We might even win the prize. It's a whole ten shilling note.'

'I don't think we're good enough.' Elfie was doubtful.

'Speak for yerself,' said Margaret, and embraced the lamp-post like a microphone. She gave a passable impression of Vera Lynn, belting out 'We'll Meet Again' at the top of her voice. 'How's that then?'

'Common, to be honest,' said Shonna. 'But it'll have to do.' She turned to Elfie. 'What about you?'

Elfie pulled her shoulders back and stared straight ahead, hands neatly folded in front of her:

> 'A little peach in an orchard grew
> A little peach of emerald hue
> Warmed by the sun and wet by the dew . . .'

Shonna held up her hand. 'Enough,' she shouted. 'That won't exactly have them rolling in the aisles, will it? Don't you know any funny poems?'

'No, I don't.'

'Then I suppose we'll have to put up with that.' Shonna put her arm round Margaret. 'I shall have to pin my hopes on you.' They ran off together and Elfie looked after them sadly. Shonna was quite wrong. 'The Little Peach' was not supposed to be funny. It was very dramatic, and made her cry. She stood in front of her mother's dressing table mirror making the right-shaped mouth for the vowel sounds, determined to do well and make Shonna proud of her. Margaret would not win. The Groutages never got anything right.

On the Friday night they presented themselves at the town hall half an hour before the show to rehearse with the pianist. In the cavernous room photographs of the Mayors of Baring-in-the-Marshes looked down with beady eyes over hooked noses and double chins, in red regalia and gold chains of office.

There were two other Vera Lynns and a jolly boy who was going to do an impression of 'Just William'. Two baby things dressed as chickens were piping 'Hey Little Hen' in a corner, while their mother looked on adoringly. Three skinny sisters appeared, faces plastered with make-up, heads topped by large spotted bows and tap-shoes on their feet as big as clogs, and had a row with the pianist about the music. A young lad arrived accompanied by his mother, owl-like spectacles on his nose and a sheaf of music under his arm. The stage manager helped him balance on a pile of cushions at the piano. He played a Beethoven Sonata beautifully.

'Now listen to that,' exclaimed Margaret. 'That's a nice little tune and don't he play it well. We won't stand an earthly now, will we?'

Shonna arrived and noticed the talented child immediately. She jerked her thumb in his direction. 'What does he do?'

'He plays the piano. He's good at it too. It reminds me of Sister Julie Anne,' said Elfie.

'Oh, he's good is he?' said Shonna and went across to his mother with a beaming smile. 'I've heard about your clever little boy,' she said, and sat down beside them on the front row. Elfie and Margaret could not hear what she was saying because the Vera Lynns were quarrelling with the dancing sisters about who should go first.

'Look at her. Queening it in the one and nines,' said Margaret bitterly. 'Making up to him ain't she? Knows he's going to win and wants to share the glory.'

They settled themselves into seats and waited for the show to start. Elfie's stomach felt full of butterflies and she kept going over 'The Little Peach' in her mind. The curtains parted to a drum roll and the compère announced 'Betty le Belle'.

A pretty girl, long legs streakily tanned with Wet White, came on and sang and danced her way through 'County Fair'. Elfie was enthralled. If only she could have dancing lessons, she was sure she would do as well. But her mother said stage people weren't nice to know, and crossed over if she saw one in the street. The girl danced off and a comedian bounced on, short and loud, in an oversize checked jacket and tight trousers. His legs kept twitching and doing funny things, they did not seem to belong to him at all. He started telling jokes.

> 'There was a young lady named Starkey.
> Went out in a jeep with a darky.
> Then for her sins, she had three sets of twins.
> Two . . .'

Elfie did not hear the rest for Margaret's raucous laughter ringing in her ears. She was glad her mother was not there. There was something about the comedian that she did not like. If only the dancing girl would come back.

An ageing couple in evening dress did some ballroom dancing after the style of Rogers and Astaire. Elfie thought it very boring, and people got up from their seats even before they had finished. It must be the interval. The girls ran to the front row to speak to Shonna, but she pretended not to know them. She was playing with the little boy and giving him chocolate from her pocket.

'Come on,' Margaret pulled Elfie away. 'We know when we're not wanted.'

Refreshments were being served at the back of the hall. Cardboard cups of lemonade and home-made biscuits, to raise money for the soldiers' comforts. The boy's mother swayed towards them carrying a tray with three cups on it and a pile of biscuits. Shonna had got herself well in. Margaret edged past the table and swiped a cup of lemonade without paying. 'Here drink this. Wet your whistle before you go on.' They shared it, and watched Shonna leading the little boy to the cloakroom to wash his sticky hands. Elfie's heart was thumping now that her turn was so close.

The music started up again and the three dancing girls did their bit. They could not keep in time with each other and the smallest one kept looking at her sisters' feet. At last they went 'shuffling off to buffalo' to lukewarm applause, blaming the pianist. Next was Shonna's new friend, his name was Maurice Bernstein. 'He should be in an internment camp with a name like that,' said Margaret venomously. The compère called Maurice Bernstein again, but the small boy appeared to have lost his glasses. He burst into tears.

'Don't worry son,' said the compère, shoving a couple of Vera Lynns on to the stage. 'You can go later.' But the spectacles could not be found, and the poor lad was taken away by his mother. She scolded him loudly for being so careless and losing his chance.

Margaret got up and did her turn. She gave it all she had got, causing the stage manager to stuff his fingers in his ears, in mock alarm. She took the top note at the end without wavering, 'SOME . . . SUNNY . . . DAY', and went off to rounds of enthusiastic applause, stamps and whistles, kissing her hand at the audience and winking at the compère.

Then it was Elfie. Her feet felt like cotton wool as she climbed the steps to the stage, and forgot all about turning her head for a better profile. She directed her voice to the back of the hall, staring straight ahead. It was then that she caught sight of Mr Creavy and the bus conductress sitting on the back row. He had his arm round her shoulders and they looked like lovers.

'A little peach in an orchard grew . . .' Elfie faltered, forgetting the next line. What if Shonna had seen them? It would upset her terribly. Elfie looked down at her, hoping for inspiration. Shonna was mouthing at her 'a little peach of emerald hue'.

'A little peach . . .' Elfie dried up completely. Shonna's green eyes were sparkling merrily from behind round tortoiseshell spectacles. Elfie ran off the stage crying. Mr Creavy and the conductress suddenly got up and left by the side door. Elfie was too upset to line up with the others for the judging. Whatever would Shonna say to her? She could have died of shame . . . that poor little boy.

Margaret won the prize and waved the ten shilling note in triumph. 'I may not be a film star after all. I think I'll be a dance band singer. You know, like that Anne Shelton.'

'Fat chance,' said Shonna, and grabbed the ten shilling note. 'I'll take charge of that.' She turned on Elfie. 'What happened to you? You made a right fool of yourself, didn't you?'

'It was when I saw you in those glasses. Oh Shonna, how could you?' Elfie started to cry all over again.

Shonna stared at her. 'Glasses? What glasses? I don't wear glasses.'

'Perhaps you ought to,' said Margaret. 'Then you'd have seen your old man on the back row with that red-haired clippie. Necking for all they were worth. They went when they saw Elfie howling. Guilty, that's what they are.' Taking advantage of Shonna's discomfort, Margaret snatched back the prize and legged it across the main road, shouting at them through the traffic, 'That'll teach you. Pinch my prize would you? Ha ha! You'll have to get up early to catch me.' She ran off and disappeared. Shonna and Elfie walked home in silence. Shonna was very angry. It was better not to talk to her in that sort of mood.

Later that evening Margaret called at Elfie's house and gave her a shilling out of the prize money. 'Do something for me,' she said.

'What?'

'Write to Victor Sylvester will you? Your spelling's better than mine. Tell him I want to be a singer with his band. Tell him I can sing and that I've won a prize. Tell him I'm very pretty too.'

Elfie hugged her. 'I'll tell him you're very nice,' she said.

That would do as well and would not be a lie. She looked at Margaret appraisingly. Her love could not quite stretch to calling her pretty.

'Ta,' said Margaret cheerfully. 'Do it in that lovely handwriting they teach you at that convent. He'll be real impressed with that. And decorate it with some music notes. I reckon me fortune is made. I'll have a dress in gold lamé with a fish-tail at the bottom. Ooh! I can see meself already. When I get real famous I'll have a microphone studded with diamonds. It'll knock Jim's eyes out. Watch out! Here comes Shonna. I'm off.'

5

Shonna was standing on her hands with her feet thrown up against the vicarage wall. Her head could not be seen because her kilt had become untucked from her knickers and had fallen over it, muffling her voice, which was announcing that stronger steps must be taken to rid her father of the bus conductress.

Elfie wished that she was supple enough to do acrobatics like Shonna. 'Shh,' she said, putting her finger on her lips and pointing at Margaret who had formed her body into a 'U' bend. With her tummy arched in the air, her ankles grasped with both hands, Margaret made her way down the path. Passers-by stared at her grotesque position.

'I shan't hush,' Shonna replied. 'It doesn't matter now. She knows, doesn't she? Saw them at the concert. What does she care.'

Margaret had taken the news of Mr Creavy's infidelity lightly. She told Shonna that if she played her cards right it could come in handy for a bit of pocket money. She often earned sixpence by keeping Molly out the way when an 'uncle' visited. Shonna had replied that she was above taking bribes. Now she said to Margaret, 'Get up. You're only showing off so that the boys can see your knickers.' Margaret jumped up, her face flushed from the exertion and hearing the truth. Shonna was, as usual, right on the button.

'What are you going to do to that conductress?' Elfie went on.

'Kill her,' Shonna said calmly. 'That's what.' She made it sound, thought Elfie, as though people did that sort of thing every day.

'The Bible says "Thou shalt not",' declared Elfie, 'And she's bigger than you, and stronger.'

'Well, I can put a spell on her,' Shonna bragged.

Margaret sniggered. 'Not another of your old spells. You weren't much good at it the last time, were you?'

Shonna ignored her. 'I know where there's a real magic book. One with proper spells in it. Ones that tell you how to summon up the Devil.'

'You've tried that before,' Margaret reminded her. 'Remember? Ouija? Scaredy pants. Frit you out of your life didn't it? You sulked and we all had to go home.'

Shonna stuck her tongue out. 'You cheated. That was why.'

Elfie feared a fight starting and tried to coax her. 'Tell us about the spell Shonna.' She hoped it would be as exciting as the night they buried the rose.

Taking a bit of chalk from her kilt pocket, Shonna made a circle on the church wall. Inside it she drew an evil-looking face with slanting eyes and a pointed beard. It looks like the cemetery goat, thought Elfie. Around the circle she wrote the letters EEJA.

'Eeja instead of Ouija this time; that's a change.' Margaret's tone was sarcastic but Shonna silenced her with a look.

'Those,' she tapped the letters, 'are important in Black Magic. They've got sinister meanings, so there.'

The vestry door opened and the vicar came out, followed by a group of choirboys in crisp white surplices, cake-frilled at the neck. Shonna stood in front of the sign and spread her arms out. 'Good morning Canon Rutherford,' she said pleasantly. 'Is there going to be a funeral?'

'Indeed not, Shonna,' he replied. 'It's a wedding we're attending. But do carry on with your game.' He departed with his entourage through the church door. Margaret, who had been exchanging glances with a choirboy, now showed signs of losing interest in the game. Shonna picked up a stick and rapped the goatish head sharply to draw her attention. 'Who's this?'

'Search me,' Margaret shrugged.

'Is it the Devil?' Elfie asked timidly.

'Good girl. Right first time.' Shonna patted her head with the stick.

'It don't look nothing like him,' said Margaret. Shonna quickly drew two small horns on the head.

'It does now.'

'But you still can't do Black Magic,' Margaret insisted. 'You've got to be a witch for that. You ain't got a long enough nose,' she fingered her own proudly, 'nor a cauldron nor even a broomstick.' She danced round Shonna chanting 'double double, toil and trouble'.

Shonna stuck out her foot and tripped her. 'Not that sort of magic, stupid. That's the fairy story kind. There is another sort you know. The kind they write about in old books. Ones with very small print. The ones they keep under the counter at the library, so children can't get them.'

'Is there things in them that we're not supposed to see?' Margaret showed a sudden interest. 'I bet they'll never let us borrow it.'

'They won't know,' said Shonna. 'We're not going to ask. Just feed Molly lots to drink and as soon as we get in there she'll ask for the lavatory. The lady's sure to take her. She won't want a puddle on the floor.'

It was all so easy. They were in and out in ten minutes with the book, and made their way to the park to read the black magic book, crawling under the bandstand because it was more exciting to read there among the spiders' webs and the white grass that never saw daylight. Shonna had brought a torch with her.

'What do you want to hear? Venereal Experiments, Infernal Necromancy or Works of Hatred and Destruction?'

'We can read the venereal bit in the public lavs,' said Margaret. 'It's on a poster there. It don't look very exciting. I'd like a bit of hatred and destruction.'

'OK, that'll probably be the bit to tell me how to deal with *her* anyway.' Shonna started to read:

'Concerning Hatred and Destruction. Experiments on enemies may be performed in different ways, but whether with some waxen image, or any other instrument, the particulars of each must be diligently and faithfully observed. Should the day or the hour fail Thee, proceed as already laid down . . .'

'Sounds boring.' Margaret yawned. 'Don't make much sense neither. Ain't there any good bits, with tombstones and things in them? You know, coffins opening and folk rising up from the dead, all covered in cobwebs.'

Shonna snapped the book shut. 'You don't understand,' she said crossly.

'Isn't there any little bits about witches or wizards?' Elfie asked.

'No. I've told you, it's not kid's stuff. It's serious. This book's been handed down from the Middle Ages. It isn't fairy tales. It's called the "Grimoire". It's powerful . . . dangerous unless you use it right. If you don't want to learn, get yourself a Grimms' fairy tale. There's plenty of witches in them.' Shonna started to crawl out from the aperture. 'I'm going to read this at home. Then I'll tell you what to do.'

'Yes. You learn all the spells,' said Margaret, 'and put one on me dad. Turn him into a frog.'

Shonna put a safe distance between herself and Margaret before shouting, 'No need, he looks like one already.'

Margaret cupped her hands to her mouth. 'Yes, but he ain't a coward like yours. He's out a-fighting for his King and country. My dad's a hero. What's yours?' Then she belted off across the park like a whippet.

When Elfie got home she asked her father about magic. 'Can people really be made to disappear?'

Mr Brown thought for a bit. 'Well there's people on stage that can do it,' he said. 'Magicians. Remember the one in the pantomime?'

'Yes.' He'd put a girl into a box and shut all the doors. Then stuck long swords through it where her head must have been, criss-crossing each other. They must have gone straight through her brain. He'd said a magic word and opened the box. The girl had vanished.

'Where did she go?' Elfie asked.

Mr Brown had a strong suspicion that she had still been in the box, but he did not want to spoil the mystery. 'It's power,' he said. 'Some people with strong characters can be very powerful. They just have to learn the right spells.'

'Do you think Shonna could learn how?'

'Shonna?' Mr Brown pretended to think. 'Yes. Now I think she'd be one of those who could do it. Oh yes. I should say so. With a bit of practice. Is she thinking of taking it up then? Making a career of it, eh?' Elfie started to reply but he held up his hand. 'Hush now. The news is on.' He sat down with his ear close to the set and twiddled the bakelite knob. Rommel was still on the run in Africa.

Later Shonna announced that they would carry out the first spell on Saturday, while her mother was out shopping at Liptons. 'Saturday,' she told them, 'is the day of Saturn. It serves well for invoking the souls in hell. Wax effigies, that's what we're going to make. We shall do things to them.' She pointed to Elfie. 'You bring some candles, and you,' to

Margaret, 'some pins. Elfie, you bring a real linen hanky too. Don't forget. It's most important.'

Elfie found some white candles in the kitchen cupboard, some pink birthday cake ones as well. They were pretty, but perhaps a bit too small to make an effigy. An effigy was a holy word for a statue so it would not matter if they were white. She put the two biggest candles in her purse along with her best embroidered hanky.

Shonna let them into the kitchen by the side door and told them not to make too much noise as her father was upstairs in bed.

'Sleeping it off?' Margaret asked pleasantly.

'No,' said Shonna, glaring at her. 'He's not full of beer like your uncles. He gets up in the night sometimes for his work and has to rest in the afternoons.'

'To get ready for the fire-watching.' Margaret slyly poked Elfie in the ribs.

'Well come on, let's get on with it.' Shonna led the way into the kitchen, a large bright room with lots of white tiling, the floor covered in blue check linoleum. Against the wall stood a pine dresser decorated with willow-pattern plates. On the table by the window stood a vase of chrysanthemums, and a fire burned brightly in the shiny black leaded grate. When I grow up, thought Elfie, I'll have a kitchen just like this and I'll clean it all day long. She gave the candles to Shonna who snatched them crossly.

'I really wanted coloured ones, pink and blue. Still I suppose these will do.' She struck a match and lit one of them, turning it upside down to drip wax on to a tin tray. Some of it ran over the edge and on to the tablecloth, and the room filled with a dreadful smell. Elfie, who was hovering close, felt her eyes start to water.

'What a pong,' said Margaret. 'Do hurry up for God's sake. You dad'll smell it.'

Shona said he did not have a good sense of smell, and added

enigmatically, 'Lucky for him, where he works.' She fashioned with wax two anaemic little figures. But when she tried to pick them up, the wax had set and they crumbled to pieces.

'Try scooping them up on a knife,' Margaret suggested.

Shonna said a cake slice might be better and attempted to slide it under them, without any success. She turned on Elfie, 'Trust your mother to buy cheap candles that fall to bits. We'll have to use something else.' She got the black magic book from under the dresser where she had hidden it, and flipped through the pages making a great pretence of consulting it. 'It says here that if you can't get wax, use Plasticine.'

'They didn't have no Plasticine in them days,' said Margaret.

Shonna did not reply, but pulled her old toy box out of the cupboard and rummaged through it until she found what she wanted. A ball of Plasticine, several colours rolled into one, making it a uniform brown shade. 'This'll do,' she said, and silently rolled it into two shapes that closely resembled ginger-bread men. She stood back to admire them. 'How's that?'

'They've got no faces,' Margaret pointed out. 'Shouldn't they have faces?'

Shonna marked eyes and mouths on them with a pencil point. 'There. Now for the ceremony. Give me the pins; we've got to stick them in the victim. In the part we want to harm. I've decided on her heart. It may just break, or she may have a heart attack. I'll let the Devil decide.'

She took one of the pins and stuck it sharply into a ginger-bread chest, then followed it by two more, just to make certain. Shonna looked quite evil all of a sudden, her face screwed up with hate. Gosh, thought Elfie, she really means it. Margaret asked, 'How will the Devil know which is which? They both look alike. He may do up the wrong one.'

Shonna frowned, and thought for a moment. Then she took a little bit of Plasticine, rolled it between her thumb and finger into a tiny sausage shape and stuck it between the legs of the pinless effigy. 'There, that'll tell him.'

Margaret got a fit of giggles. Elfie whispered to her, 'What's that?'

'Ah! You wouldn't know, would you. You ain't got brothers, have you? It's his little dangler.'

'Shut up,' Shonna shouted. 'Can't you see I'm trying to concentrate.' She picked up the two figures and placed them side by side on Elfie's hanky and wrapped them up. Then she went into the pantry and returned with a large cardboard box which she placed on top of the cooker. 'The altar,' she explained.

'Says Swan Vestas,' said Margaret. 'Don't say that on our altar up the chapel.'

Shonna turned it round. The kitchen was getting darker now; a few drops of rain pattered on the window panes. Shonna drew the magic circle on the kitchen floor in red chalk, stuck the other candle in a saucer and lit it. It sputtered a bit and then burned feebly. She went over to the grate and scraped a spoonful of soot off the back of the chimney and threw it over the flame. It seemed to go out for a second then rose higher with a fizz and black smoke threatened the curtains.

'We're on fire!' yelled Elfie. Shonna snatched the flower vase and hurled it over the candle. It expired with a weak hiss; the chrysanthemums lay scattered on the floor. Blackened water flowed off the table. Shonna ordered them to kneel down, saying 'Let us pray'.

'Better pray your dad don't come down and catch us,' laughed Margaret, looking at the mess.

Shonna was chanting, 'In the name of the Father and of the Son and of the Holy Ghost. Take heed. Come all ye spirits. By the virtue and power of your King, all spirits of the Hells are forced to appear in my presence, before this circle of Solomon.' She tapped the circle with the spoon, leaving a black mark. 'Come then! Fulfil that which is in Thy power. Come from the East, South, West and North!'

'North, South, East and West,' Elfie corrected.

'You shut up. I've got it right.' Shonna raised her arms above her head. The rain was lashing down now and the kitchen was getting quite dark. Elfie shifted nearer to Margaret, while Shonna went on, 'Most Holy Adonai who liveth and reigneth forever.'

'Amen,' said Elfie, crossing herself. Shonna reached out and smacked her round the ear.

'Don't do that. The Devil doesn't like it.'

Margaret was laughing, loud guffaws that made her lose her breath. 'Where is he then? I can't see him.'

'Behind you!' Shonna shouted.

Margaret got up and jumped forward in mock alarm, look-ing behind her and clutching her bottom. 'He's got me on his prongs,' she giggled.

'Get out!' screeched Shonna. 'Get out the pair of you!'

Margaret carried on, jerking and laughing towards the door. On the way, Elfie saw her pick up a pin and stick it straight through the hanky, right on the spot where Shonna had placed the dangler. 'That'll fix him,' she said. They ran out into the rain and Shonna threw their coats after them.

'Don't ever come back,' she screamed. 'The Devil will not be mocked.'

'She's batty.' Margaret pulled Elfie along the road. 'Put your coat over your head. I reckon she'll end up like her dad. They say he's a bit of a rum one.'

'But do you think the spell will work?'

'No,' said Margaret. 'Hers won't, but mine will. I reckon I've got the power.' She spread her fingers out, stabbing them in the air. 'I've put the 'fluence on him.'

Three days later she was saying to Elfie, 'Told you so. Her old man's in the hospital.' She lowered her voice. 'Got a rupture.'

'What's that?'

'Summit to do with your privates. Me grandpa had one for

years. Had to wear a sort of string bag to keep his bits in. Mr Creavy won't be doing any fire-watching for a bit. Still, I bet Shonna'll take the credit and say it were all her work. But we know the truth, don't we? You saw where I put the pin. Whatever she does, I can do better. I've gone off her anyway. Last night she called at our house and gave me mum a parcel, and said "Here you are. Alms for the poor". Me mum opened it and out fell all them Creavys's old clothes.'

'What did your mother say?'

'Called her a cheeky little bugger. Flung a shoe at her. Said "We don't want none of your cast-offs."'

'Of course you don't,' Elfie agreed. 'You don't want their old clothes.'

'I'd have just liked a pair of shoes, Elf. Even if they were Shonna's. Just look at me feet.'

Elfie looked down to where Margaret's toes poked through Tom's old boots. She was right. Any shoes were better than none. Margaret saw her looking and said proudly, 'Never mind. When I'm grown up I'll have shoes with ten inch high heels, lots of them, at least twenty pairs, and a cigarette holder . . . and pink silk camiknickers . . . when I get to be a woman. When my "country cousins" come.'

Shonna and Elfie sat on the park bench and waited for Margaret to join them. Only a week now till Christmas, and the wintry sun shone on the frozen lake where a few brave souls were skating regardless of the cracks in the ice.

'I wish we had skates,' said Elfie wistfully. 'It looks such fun.' She pictured herself and Shonna gliding over the ice together, hand in hand. Margaret arrived, out of breath and looking excited. She did not sit down but stood awkwardly in front of them, looking as though she had something important to say. As though sensing it, Shonna ignored her. 'We could make a slide,' she said to Elfie. 'That would be almost as good.'

'I can't,' said Margaret, 'not today.' Curiosity got the better of Shonna. 'Why not?'

'Can't put me feet on the ice, in case the blood rushes to me head and kills me.'

'What on earth are you jabbering about?' said Shonna.

Margaret took on a new, important air. Puffed up with pride she told them, 'I've become a woman.' She looked at them expectantly as though hoping for a round of applause.

Shonna eyed her disdainfully. 'So what? I've been one for ages. It doesn't stop me going on the ice. What rubbish have they told you?'

'Well, I mustn't put me feet on a cold floor. And I mustn't go in the sea, or wash me hair, or have a bath.'

'Then you'll stink,' said Shonna. 'That's just old wives' tales. Only common people believe them. My mother says her Ladyship at the Big House where she worked took five baths a day, and six at certain times of the month.'

'Well mark my words,' Margaret uttered darkly. 'My Aunty Shirley knew this girl and she went in the sea when she had her monthlies. Sank straight to the bottom and were never seen again. 'Scuse me. I must sit down. Makes yer feel all weak.' She flicked some snow off the bench and placed her bottom down very carefully.

'You're talking nonsense,' Shonna told her. 'Is that all?'

'Well, there were something else as well.' Margaret dropped her voice and they had to bend close to hear her. 'If you go with a man and he gives you a baby, it gets caught up in the blood and comes out with big red patches on it. You know, you've seen them.'

Fascinated, they jostled for position next to her on the bench. Elfie won. She thought about the boy they knew in Arcadia Road who had such a patch over his eye. Her mother had told her it was a port wine stain. Nonsense. It was nothing of the sort. Her mother would be ashamed to speak the truth. It was not very nice. Might be better to avoid the boy in future. She asked Margaret, 'Did your Aunty Shirley tell you everything . . . like she promised?'

'Yes. Only I'm not going to tell you, cos you're only a little girl.'

Margaret got up and went and sat next to Shonna, cupping her hands and whispering in her ear. They gave shrieks of horror and clutched at each other, falling to the ground. Margaret forgot her new womanhood for a moment and rolled about laughing uncontrollably. When she remembered, she clambered to her feet and self-consciously pulled her skimpy skirt down over her knees.

'You didn't see anything, did you?' she asked Elfie.

'No,' said Elfie, not quite sure what she was supposed to have seen.

Margaret turned to Shonna, excluding Elfie from the conversation. 'So I asked me Aunty Shirley, see, if it hurt. And she said, "Only if they don't leave the money on the mantelpiece."' They both started giggling again, until tears came into their eyes. 'She said, "No larking about with boys and no French kissing, it leads to babies."'

Elfie pushed herself in between them, her round innocent face looking up into theirs. 'Please, what is French kissing?'

'Haven't you seen it on the films?' Margaret sounded surprised. 'Cooh! They do it all the time. That Tyrone Power, he's real good at it. They bend the woman over backwards and then stick their tongues down their throats. It's full of passion.' She bent Elfie over backwards to demonstrate.

'I don't think I'd like it,' said Elfie, pulling away. Secretly she thought she was not going to have much chance of meeting a film star, and Peter Collins had so far shown no such inclination, though once he had held her hand under the desk at school. It might just be worth it if there was a little baby at the end. A cuddly bundle like June had been. Lost in a daydream of holding the baby close to her and hearing it gurgle, a tear ran unchecked down Elfie's cheek. Margaret looked at her.

'What are you crying for Elf? Don't worry. We won't let it happen to you. It's only for us grown-up girls. You'd better tell your dad to watch out, Shonna. He were in the flicks last night. French kissing with that red-haired clippie. He hardly saw the film at all. Don't he know it's dangerous? She could have a baby.'

'If she does, I'll kill it.'

Two pairs of eyes stared at her in horror. Kill a baby! That was really mean. Elfie started bawling out loud. 'You wouldn't talk of killing babies if you'd seen one die.'

'You didn't,' said Shonna. 'Your baby died in the hospital.'

'But I saw her when they brought her home. She was put in the parlour with candles by the table. Daddy held my hand and took me in to see her. She was all white and still. I couldn't believe that she had ever been real. Please . . . please . . . don't let's talk about killing babies.'

Margaret tried to comfort her. 'She's got a nice little grave, Elf. And all the babies have pretty little white coffins. They treat them real good. Me Aunty Shirley says that even if they're stillborn and have never drawn a breath they gets popped into a coffin wiv a grown-up. So they can get looked after like, and get a good Christian burial. And she must like the flowers you take her every week.'

Until then, Elfie had not really thought very much about where June might have gone, only that she missed her terribly. A new picture came into her mind. The white cross, so dumpy in size, looked like a child with outstretched arms. Perhaps Margaret was right, and June was in there. Perhaps all the people who had died were in their gravestones, waiting for the trumpet to sound. There were big granite crosses for the men and roundish stones that looked like old ladies with shawls over their heads for the women. It was a comforting thought. She squeezed Margaret's hand gratefully and sniffed loudly.

Shonna looked at her in disgust. 'Your bladder is too near

your eyeballs. Are we going to listen all day to your bleating, or are we going to play something?'

'Let her choose. We'll play what she wants today,' Margaret said.

So they played the parcel game, Elfie's favourite. Shonna wrapped up a stone in brown paper and tied it with string into an intriguing-looking parcel. They attached a reel of thread to it and placed it at the end of the alley. Shonna hid around the corner holding the reel, and Elfie and Margaret watched from the far side of the street. When someone put out a hand to pick it up they gave Shonna the signal and she jerked the string. The parcel disappeared up the alley. It amused them for hours, having a slight element of danger about it. One day someone might chase them – and who knew what could happen if you were caught by a stranger. Today there were few people about, it was so cold, and Shonna soon tired of the game and went wandering off up the alleyway, leaving the parcel unattended. They saw her in the distance peering over Mrs Tew's fence. The evacuees were not there any more. They had gone back to London, much preferring the bombs to Shonna's bows and arrows. Mrs Tew came out of the back door and shook her fist. Elfie wondered if she blamed Shonna for the loss of the children. Suddenly Margaret grabbed Elfie by the hand.

'Look!' she exclaimed, as her face had turned white. 'Look at that. A ghost!'

'I didn't see anything,' whispered Elfie. 'Only Mrs Tew.'

'Well I did. I saw a hand waving from the undertaker's window. Shonna waved back,' said Margaret.

'Maybe it's someone she knows.'

'Oh yes? Pale as that hand, and seven foot up? I hope it weren't a corpse. I hope she's not trying to raise the dead!' They shivered together in delicious fright.

6

Elfie felt the best thing about Christmas, apart from opening her stocking, was Midnight Mass. It was holy and exciting, with the incense giving her a funny feeling like being dizzy. It meant staying up late and going out in the dark. They always went to the big cathedral in the city, where you had to be early if you wanted a seat in the pews. Now it was wartime, more people than ever were going to pray for the soldiers overseas.

This year, however, Elfie was looking forward to it a bit less than usual, because Shonna had asked her if she could go with them. Instead of feeling happy at being able to do her friend a favour, Elfie was worried. Since stealing the black magic book Shonna had shown quite a morbid interest in Catholic things, and Elfie felt it was not quite right for Shonna to pry into a religion which she had always professed to despise. She asked the oddest questions. One day she had questioned Elfie about the colour of the mass.

Masses did not come in colours. Everyone should know that. You couldn't see them, only hear them. If you wanted one said for you, it cost a penny and the priest lit a little candle. These were stuck into coloured pots. Maybe that's what Shonna meant. Elfie answered, 'Red, green or blue.'

Shonna had looked disappointed. 'No black ones?'

'No,' Elfie had replied firmly. 'No black ones.' Then she had told her, 'You can't come on Christmas Eve because you're not a Catholic. You're not confirmed either.'

'That's all right. I won't take communion. I'll just sit in the pew while you all go up. No one will mind.' Elfie shook her head. Shonna looked determined. 'If you don't let me go I'll tell your mother you walk home with Peter Collins. I'll tell her your name's chalked on the lavatory wall with his, E.B. loves P.C.'

'It isn't,' said Elfie. 'You know it isn't.'

'But does your mother know it isn't? Is she going in there to look?'

Elfie gave in reluctantly and asked her mother, saying, 'Please let her. She is my best friend.'

Mrs Brown said that was a pity, and she could not see for the life of her why Shonna wanted to go as she was practically a heathen. Only last week Mrs Creavy had been sent for by Sister Ignatious because Shonna had said that she could not believe in the Immaculate Conception with Joseph around. Such a cheek! Mrs Brown ranted on about it until her husband put down his newspaper and said, 'Kids say these things. It's all a bit of bravado. I can't see any harm in it, Doris. It'll be company for Elfie. I expect Shonna only wants to stay up late like the others. Let her go.'

Elfie wondered what Shonna was up to. She was always plotting something, wasn't she? She had never asked to go with them before. What if she misbehaved? Showed them all up? Her mother would kill her. Perhaps she would catch the measles and that would keep her at home.

On Christmas Eve there was Shonna, the picture of health, dressed in a bright red cloth coat nipped in at the waist, with a white fur collar and hat to match. To complete the outfit she carried a muff. Elfie knew she could not compete. Her own Sunday coat was a serviceable tweed with a half belt and a box pleat at the back, which Mummy said was ladylike and made her look like the little Princesses. I don't want to look like them, Elfie thought. Elizabeth is fat like me, and the little one has a big nose. Anyway, I want to look like Shonna; she's my friend.

They piled into the car. Shonna sat in the back with Elfie, but kept leaning forward to make conversation with Mrs Brown, who answered in monosyllables, scarcely concealing her dislike of the girl. While Mr Brown parked the car, they made their way to the cathedral with the throngs of other worshippers. Elfie looked up at the sky and half hoped a bomber would appear and make everyone run for their lives. That would be exciting. But apart from the new moon and a few scattered stars, the sky was clear. The huge porchway was in darkness when they arrived, with no festive lights and no decorated tree. Surely the Germans would not be mean enough to bomb a Christmas tree.

Lurking in the shadows at the edge of the crowd was a ragged-looking man, leaning against one of the pillars. His unkempt beard fell to his chest in two matted strands, his clothes were in tatters and his eyes wild and staring. Elfie shrank up against her mother as they passed. Shonna saw him too, and swivelled her head round boldly for another look, earning herself a reproving glare from Mrs Brown.

They found an empty pew near the back and filed into it, Shonna and Elfie first, then Mr and Mrs Brown. They sank to their knees to pray, and Elfie peeped out through her fingers to see if everything was the same as last year and all the years before. Seasonal music floated down from the organ loft, the intense young man at the keys hunching his shoulders, his eyes closed, carried away by his own playing. There was the crib that she had helped to decorate; the Infant Jesus had a chipped nose where she had dropped him on the floor. She hoped no one would notice, and said a little prayer asking God to make her less clumsy next year.

Just before the service began, the shabby man came sham-
bling in, pushing himself into the row in front of them.
Everybody had to move up to make room, noses poked in the
air, offended by the acrid smell of stale urine that accompanied
him. Shonna pinched her nose with her fingers and Mr Brown
shook his head disapprovingly at her. She got up and pushed
past them rudely, as though she was in the cinema, and sat
directly behind the tramp to get a better look.

The priest entered by the chancel door. An altar boy following swung the incense container wildly, trying to compose his
cheeky face into an expression of holiness. The smell of the
incense obliterated that of the old man. Elfie peeped round
her parents to see if Shonna was joining in the service, but her
mother pushed her back irritably. Bad behaviour seemed to
be catching, but Elfie had seen that Shonna's mouth was not
moving and that she was holding her hymn book upside down.
She was staring, her eyes fixed and unblinking, on the back
of the poor man.

The collection plate was passed around and reached the row
in front of them. Elfie could see among the coins a bright new
halfcrown. Gosh! Someone was rich tonight. God would be
pleased with that. The plate reached the raggedy man. He
fumbled in his pocket then shook his head, refusing to take
it. His neighbour passed it back to Shonna, who turned away
so as not to let them see what she was putting in.

'Hurry up. You're keeping everyone waiting,' Mrs Brown
chided her, snatching the plate and dropping a threepenny bit
in it. Mr Brown put a shilling in and gave the plate to Elfie.
The halfcrown had disappeared. It must have fallen to the
bottom amongst the pennies. What a pity as she would have
liked a better look at it. Elfie carefully dropped in a sixpence
that she had been saving for weeks. The organ started
up again with a chesty, wheezing sound. She forgot about
the collection and started to sing 'O infant Jesus, Child
divine, we consecrate our hearts to Thee', while thinking

'Please God, don't let her do anything naughty and show us up.'

'To burn fo-or souls wi-ith zeal like Thine . . .'

Shonna's eyes were burning, right into the back of the old man. Were little sparks coming from them like fireworks? Or was it the candles flickering?

Now they were lining up for communion, leaving Shonna behind in the pew. The old man stayed there too. When Elfie's turn came she knelt at the altar rail between her parents, feeling very devout, and put out her tongue. It was funny, but this was the only time you could put out your tongue without being rude. The priest lifted the chalice above his head with both hands and blessed the wine, then sped down the row giving everyone but the children a sip. He had just reached Mrs Brown when there was a strangled cry from the back of the church, followed by a dreadful gargling sound. Was it Shonna? Was she falling on the ground clutching her throat? Oh, the shame. They would never be able to come here again. Elfie sneaked a look. Shonna was sitting exactly where they had left her, hands decorously inside the muff. The priest carried on as though nothing had happened.

As she walked back to her seat Elfie could see the old man lying on the ground, limbs flailing. As she got nearer she could see flecks of foam on his lips, a trickle of water running from under him. He must be ill. How silly of her to think it might have been Shonna. The man was picked up and carried out now by the verger and a member of the congregation. Elfie found she could not get rid of the communion wafer. It had stuck to the roof of her mouth. How could you swallow it without a drink? They were mean not to let children have wine.

The priest sped up the aisle anxious to get home to bed, blessing them as he went. 'Nomine Patris, Fili et Spiritus Sancti.' He had to be up again at six in the morning. Elfie followed Shonna out, losing sight of her parents in the crush.

'That was fun, wasn't it?' said Shonna gleefully. 'Did you see him lying on the floor in a heap?'

'That wasn't funny,' said Elfie. 'He was ill.'

'Nonsense! Of course he wasn't. Didn't you see me put the 'fluence on him.'

'What for? We don't even know him.'

'I used him,' Shonna declared proudly. 'In one of the most important black magic rites. Disturbing the Midnight Mass. You just think hard about what you want to happen and it does. I nearly got it perfect. But just for one thing. He should have jumped up and shouted "Let the dead rise from their graves". It says so in the book. I can show you. Anyway, I'm getting better at it all the time. Upset everything, didn't I? And nobody knows it was me.'

'*I* know,' said Elfie, 'and *God* knows. He sees everything, and you spoiled his Christmas Mass. I wouldn't like to be you on Judgement Day.'

'It doesn't matter, so there! I don't believe in him so he can't do a thing to me.'

Outside in the porch they saw the man again, this time sitting on one of the stone benches by the wall. Mr Brown was bending over him with a cup of water. Other people were gathering round murmuring sympathetically 'such a shame . . . how sad . . . especially at Christmas.'

Shonna darted from Elfie's side and pushed through the throng of people. Kneeling down in front of the man, she looked around, aware of the pretty picture she made. 'You poor man,' her green eyes filled with tears, 'take this for a cup of tea.'

'How sweet,' said a lady in the crowd. 'What a lovely girl.'

Shonna reached into the muff, then threw a coin onto his lap. A bright shiny halfcrown.

7

Drops of blood from Shonna's finger trickled very slowly on to the snow that lay melting on the back lawn, becoming furred at the edges as though on blotting paper, and forming tiny flower patterns around the holes that always appear when snow starts to melt.

They stood watching it and Shonna gave her finger a little squeeze to make it run faster. The snowman seemed to be watching too, with beady eyes made from Elfie's mother's hatpins. A last look before he melted away. The scarf they had draped round his neck had fallen to his waist and his pipe was lying on the ground. His once crisp and rounded figure had taken on a silvery ethereal look, and little rivulets of water ran from him down the garden path.

'Oh do hurry up,' said Elfie. 'Please.' She did not want to be there when he died and became just a little heap on the ground. Shonna grabbed her and took hold of her finger, pricking it with a needle and making her squeal, then she put both their fingers together, mingling their blood. How much darker hers is, thought Elfie, it must surely be richer than mine.

'There you are. It's done. We're blood brothers now.'

'Brothers?' Elfie wondered.

'It's just an expression, silly. It means complete loyalty. I've chosen you as my special friend. Just like a real sister. I'm going to tell you my most secret thoughts and plans, and you will obey my commands. If you don't I shall consider myself betrayed and get someone else. Then I'll never speak to you again and I'll make sure no one else does either.' Elfie glowed with pride. Now she need never feel lonely again, as long as she did what Shonna told her, of course. The long hours when her mother would not speak to her would be quite bearable now.

'Of course I'll do what you tell me,' Elfie agreed eagerly. 'Anything . . . only . . . not French kissing. You won't ask me to do that, will you?'

'No, stupid. Of course not. I'm not interested in that sort of thing. What we're going to do is practise black magic and get really good at it. I want you to think of me as a sort of priest. You'll be my helper, my altar boy. You know, like in your church. There's something I shall need and you can get it for me. It's important. You can serve me when I do the spells. Don't go telling Margaret, she's sure to spoil it. She thinks she's grown up now and will try to boss us about. We'll tell her when we're ready. Understand? Right now it's just you and me. Watch out, here she comes.'

Shonna broke off as Margaret turned into the garden, teetering about on her mother's high heels, heron-like legs thrust nakedly into shoes that were at least two sizes too big. A costume jacket, the shoulders standing out as though the coat-hanger had been left in, covered a thin summer dress that nearly reached her ankles. Along with these borrowed plumes she had assumed a new grown-up air. She asked them if they would like her to take them for a walk in the park.

'No,' said Shonna. 'What do you think we are? Kids? You're not taking us walkies. Anyway it's Sunday and the monkey parade will be out. I don't want to be seen round there. It gives you a bad name. So there.'

'Suit yerself,' retorted Margaret. 'End up an old maid. See if I care.'

'I'm only twelve,' Shonna pointed out. 'Anyway, I have a lover. I told you. A secret one. I don't need to prance around the bandstand making sheep's eyes at fellows. I've got mine. Elfie's going to get one soon, too.'

'Am I?' asked Elfie.

'Yes, you are,' Shonna replied firmly, and then looked back to Margaret. 'So you can shove off. We've got better things to do.'

Margaret turned on the spiky heels, her narrow shoulders hunched under the enormous jacket. Shonna called after her, 'You'll end up a trollop like your mother.'

Margaret stopped abruptly and turned. She came back with her head down, charging like an angry bull, tripping a bit in the borrowed shoes. She flew at Shonna and pushed her into the snowman. His head rolled off.

'You leave me mum out of this. She's better than your'n. Your'n were only in service. And your dad got her in the club. Everyone knows. He were cut off with a shilling.'

Shonna righted herself quickly. Her hand flew across Margaret's pasty face and left an angry red mark. Margaret rubbed at the stinging place. 'See! You know it's true. That's why you're mad. I may be poor but I'm not a bastard like you.' Her mouth took on an ugly twist. 'Bastard! Bastard! Bastard!'

Shonna had spitefulness honed down to a fine art. She laughed. 'Yes. I am. And I don't care who knows it. At least I'm a rich little bastard. My father wasn't cut off with a shilling. He was bought off by his family, with more money than you'll ever see in your whole life. So there! You haven't even got proper shoes, and your knickers have holes in them. And skid marks.'

Margaret thrust her chin in the air and turned to go. It was no good arguing, when the whole world knew about your shoes . . . and your dirty knickers. Elfie watched her walk away, coat-hanger shoulders shaking slightly, and desperately wanted to run after her to comfort her. But the thought of Shonna's wrath, and the loss of blood brother status, deterred her. Margaret had to be sacrificed.

Shonna turned to her. 'Just forget it will you.' She waved her hand airily. 'There's much more interesting things to do than chase boys. Listen, I'm going to teach you to cause the appearance of a gentleman in your room after supper.'

'A lover?' Elfie asked hopefully.

'Doubtful at your age. But he will sit and talk to you and answer any questions you wish to ask him.'

'What if my mother sees him? Is he a ghost?'

'Yes, sort of. She won't see him. He'll only be visible to you, and at midnight he'll depart without you even having to tell him to go.'

Shonna fetched the magic book from the house, wrapped up in an antimacassar, pulled Elfie over to the garden seat, opened it at a page she had dog-eared, and started to read:

'You must prepare your chamber as soon as it is morning, and do it in such a way that it will not be liable to derangement for the rest of the day. There must be no hangings nor anything set crosswise. No tapestries, clothes, hats, birdcages or etceteras. Above all put clean sheets on the bed. Fast all day and after a light supper pass in secret to your chamber and kindle a good fire. Place a white cloth on the table and set in front of it a chair. On the table place a wheaten roll and a glass of fresh clear water. Then retire to bed uttering the following:

"Besticitum consolatio veni ad me vertet Creon. Cantor laudem omnipotentis et non commentur. Stat superior carte bient lauden omviestra principiem da montem et inimicos meos prostantis vobis et mihi dantes que passium fieri sincisbus."'

'I'll never remember all that. Is it Latin? We don't do that till we're eleven.'

Shonna ripped the page out and gave it to Elfie. 'Here, have it. I don't suppose it'll be missed. I might not take the book back anyway. Make sure you learn it, and don't lose it, and do please try to get it right.'

'I will Shonna, I promise.' Elfie skipped off home full of thoughts for her preparations. Clean sheets of course would be out of the question. Beds were changed once a fortnight when the Chinese laundry called. She would just have to 'top to bottom' them as her mother sometimes did, and hope the gentleman would not notice. He was not going to get in the bed, was he? He might have to make do with a slice of bread and Marmite instead of a wheaten roll, too.

Shonna called after her, 'Don't forget to leave your window open, so he can get in.'

Elfie woke every hour to see if it was time to get up. She had no alarm clock and feared that if she did not rise early enough, there would not be time to get it all ready before she went to school. When six o'clock came her eyes felt dry and prickly from lack of sleep. She threw off the bedclothes and, pattering quietly about the room, put a stool by the bed and stood on it whilst she stripped off all the sheets and blankets. The lumpy feather mattress, denuded of its cover, lay like a dead zebra as she panted with the exertion of getting the whole thing back together again. The most difficult bit being stuffing the bolster back inside its long thin case. Elfie hoped her mother would not notice the seams being on the wrong side. When she had finished it all looked quite fresh and neat.

Then Elfie looked around the rest of the room. What was it Shonna had said? Her brow furrowed as she tried to remember. Things set crosswise. Yes. That was it. Would not crosswise depend on which way you were going? North to South would be the way to travel. Her father always told her that people going in that direction had the right of way. She would have to hope the gentleman knew about that too, and looked out of the window to check the position with the halt sign outside. The old iron bedstead and the wardrobe were pointing in the right direction, thank goodness for that. There was no way she could have moved them, but the dressing table was wrong. It definitely stood East to West, sat squat and ugly at right angles to the bed. Elfie had always disliked it because it shut out the light. Now she put her shoulder under its ledge and heaved, getting a blow on the head from the swinging mirror. The dressing table had not moved an inch. She put her tongue out at it and rubbed her sore head. Would the gentleman be put off, and refuse to come in? What about a note, explaining. Tearing a page out of her exercise book she wrote:

Dear Mr Gentleman,
    I hope you find everything to your liking. I'm sorry about the dressing table, but I did my best. Please call if you can. Love Elfie.

She wondered if she should add a few kisses, but Shonna had been quite firm about him not being a lover, and he might think she was a bit forward. Better leave the kisses out. Elfie took her Sunday hat off the bedpost and stuffed it into the wardrobe. Now, no hanging things or drapes. The curtains? Too risky. Mummy would notice. Better to leave them alone. She had no tapestries, birdcages or etceteras, whatever they were, to worry about, so she pinned the note to the back of the dressing table and crept quietly downstairs, pretending to have breakfasted early, by sprinkling some crumbs on a plate and pouring a little milk into the bottom of her mug. She set off for school, her heart pounding with excitement.

    Peter Collins, as usual, ran down the road, eager to walk to school with her. This morning she looked at him in a new light and compared him to the gentleman of her dreams. He did not shape up at all. She wondered if a beard would ever grow on those shiny apple cheeks. It was very doubtful.

'Can I sit with you in Assembly today?' he asked.

'No, not today Peter. I'm going to sit with Shonna. We've got important things to talk about.'

'Such as?' he asked scornfully.

Elfie eyed him warily, wondering if he could keep a secret. He was a bit of a babbler, and might not understand.

Peter continued, 'You always play with her. It's not fair. You never play with me now. She's a bully, and she's mean. She told my kid brother there was no Father Christmas last year.' He thought for a bit. 'I hate her.'

Elfie made up her mind. He was too young. She was glad herself that Shonna had helped her put such childish things away. Shonna was quite right. Grown-ups should not fool little children. They only got disappointed later. His brother should be thankful.

In the assembly hall the children were already lining up, rustling prayer books and shuffling their feet. Sister Ignatious strode like a man to the platform, smacking heads with her Bible as she passed and shouting for silence, each word punctuated by a clack of the bell.

'Hail Mary, full of grace.'

'The Lord is with Thee,' the children responded in meaningless voices.

'Blessed art Thou amongst women will Elfreda Brown please stand still and blessed is the fruit of Thy womb, Jesus . . .'

Elfie stopped threading herself through the row of children and bowed her head devoutly with the others, but out of the corner of her eye could see Shonna smirking at her and knew she was being teased. They filed out of the hall after prayers and she felt someone blowing softly down her neck. She turned round and found Shonna right behind her.

'Why didn't you sit next to me?'

Shonna did not speak, but thrust a package into her hand. Elfie waited to see if anyone was looking before opening it.

Inside was a crusty roll, still a bit warm from the oven, and smelling delicious. 'For me?'

'No, silly. It's for your gentleman. I knew you wouldn't be able to get one. Put it on the table tonight.'

'Thank you.' Elfie turned into the classroom, but unable to put her mind to the lessons she got a detention, and had to stand in the Dunce's corner for a whole hour. Well at least it gave her time to think about what she could say to the gentleman, if he came of course. She thought she might ask him about the scholarship, and if Margaret would be a film star. It might be a good idea to find out too if poor Molly would ever be able to learn to read and write. When the bell went for midday break she dashed down the corridor to find Shonna, and found her sitting in the cloakroom munching cheese rolls. 'Are you sure you're fasting?' she asked Elfie.

'I haven't had anything at all. I'm very hungry. The book did say I could have a light supper didn't it?' Elfie was worried that her tummy would be making grumbling noises by the time the man arrived. That would be very embarrassing.

'Have you thought of any good questions?'

Elfie told her, but Shonna replied that she did not think much to them. Boring old questions; could she think of anything better?

'Such as what do the nuns wear under their habits. We've always wanted to know. Ask about babies too. How they get in. Oh . . . and ask him what Margaret does with Jimmy Day down the Anderson shelter.' The bell rang and Shonna went off to her classroom. Elfie did not think she could ask him any of those things. Why, he might not even know Jimmy Day. She would have to phrase the questions carefully so as not to seem cheeky.

Elfie arrived home looking very flushed. Her mother felt her forehead. 'Feverish,' she exclaimed. There had been diphtheria about. She held Elfie's tongue down with the back of a spoon and looked down her throat until Elfie gagged. 'Say ah. How lucky you've been innoculated.'

Her temperature was a little higher than normal, so Mrs Brown lit a fire in the bedroom and sent her up early to be on the safe side. That was a piece of luck. Put up to bed and a fire in the grate. The gentleman would be pleased. Elfie lay on the lumpy feather mattress and stared right into the flames. There was a figure there that looked like him, with red breeches and a smoke-plume hat, a cavalier from history. He would look like that because the magic book was very old. She stared till her eyes felt hot and gritty. Dozing off, she felt weightless. Elfie felt as if she came out of her body and floated to the ceiling, hovered there and looked down on the bed with herself still tucked up inside it. Didn't she look small. Then her heart missed a beat and she plummeted down again, remembering that she had not recited the magic words. Elfie got out of bed and felt in her pocket for the paper. It was still there, crunched up, but readable. She ran to the window and threw it open wide, letting in a blast of cold air that made the flames flatten and cringe against the firebricks.

The strange-sounding words flew out into the night, 'dantes que passium fieri sincisbus.' She added for luck, 'And God bless Daddy and Mummy and little baby June. Amen.' Climbing back to bed again Elfie fell into a restless sleep, tossing about, and dreaming of a man stepping out of the fire, as tall as Mr Creavy, and all in black. He came towards her and bent over the bed, and that was funny because it was not Mr Creavy at all. It was Peter Collins. 'Elfie,' he said, and put out his hand to touch her. She woke up with a start. A strange man *was* standing by her bed. Could it really be him? Her gentleman. Her cavalier. He was nothing like she had imagined. This man was small and balding, and his face had all the features squashed in the middle. Hardly handsome, and if she never found a lover he would not do. Now he was putting his hand on the bedclothes and trying to pull them back. Surely he was not trying to get in. She clutched them tighter to her chin.

'Go away please. You're not what I wanted.'

Her mother bobbed up from behind him. Now what was she doing there? She was not supposed to be able to see him. He put a briefcase on the table, making no attempt to eat the crusty roll. Then he put his hand on her head.

'Don't touch me, please.'

Her mother flushed. 'Do excuse her. She's delirious. Not herself at all.'

'It may be that she's more used to my partner,' he replied. 'Her face is very red. I don't like the look of her.'

Well, Elfie did not much like the look of him either. It might be a good idea to get the questions asked, then he could go. She sat bolt upright in the bed and felt giddy.

'I've been waiting to ask if I'll pass the scholarship.'

Her mother stepped forward and gently pushed her down on the pillows. 'It isn't the School Board,' she said.

Elfie raised herself up again. 'And where do babies come from?'

'Oh my goodness, what is she going to ask next?' Mrs Brown turned to the gentleman with an uncomfortable smile. 'I'm so sorry. Where do they get these questions from?'

The gentleman put up his hand to silence her. 'Don't worry, Mrs Brown. I get asked that question by lots of little girls. Always give a simple explanation suitable to their years.' He turned to Elfie, 'They come in black bags like this one. I've got one in here now that I'm taking to its mother. When you grow up perhaps I'll bring one for you.'

He was not speaking the truth. Thanks to her friends she knew enough to recognize a downright lie. All grown-ups were the same. He was no different, even if he was a gentleman and a ghost. It was very disappointing. She started to snivel, and he handed her a hanky from the pile of clean ones on the dressing-table. Well, that was kind of him. Perhaps she could get to like him just a little bit in time. The hall clock was striking twelve. Then he left by the door, and that was not right because he should have gone out of the window. Whatever would she tell Shonna? Her head felt terrible and she lay back on the pillows and fell asleep. Her mother wakened her with two yellow pills on a saucer. 'Here, take these dear, you're not very well.' She picked up the glass of water and held it out.

'Don't touch that. It belongs to my gentleman.'

'I'm sure he won't mind.' Her mother tucked the bedclothes in. 'Just drink up like a good girl, and you'll soon feel better.'

When the isolation period was over, Shonna called round to see Elfie and was let in rather grudgingly by Mrs Brown, who said, 'Don't stay too long, or get her excited. She's been quite ill, you know.'

Shonna ran her finger up the bannister rail, leaving a line snaking in the dust. 'Do you do that in your own house?' asked Mrs Brown.

'We don't have dust,' Shonna replied. Mrs Brown gave her a shove in the back that catapulted her into the bedroom, then slammed the door.

'Your mother!' Shonna told Elfie. 'Mopes all day and does nothing, then gets sniffy when she's criticized.'

'I hope you haven't made her cross, she won't let me out to play if you have. What have you said?'

'Nothing. Never mind.' Shonna sat down on the bed. 'Just tell me what happened that night. Did *he* come?'

'Yes,' said Elfie cautiously. She had made up her mind to make it sound exciting. But she was not going to tell deliberate lies.

'Well, come on . . . spit it out. Was he handsome?'

'He was a bit . . . I mean, he was very charming. He had a lovely voice.'

'You lucky beggar. Did you ask him about the nuns? You

know, what they wear and all that?' Elfie shook her head.
Shonna's face fell. 'You mean you didn't ask him? Why not?'

'Well . . . he was a real gentleman. Anyway my mother was
there,' Elfie added accusingly. 'You said she wouldn't be able
to see him.'

'What a waste. I wish I'd done it myself now. If it had been
me,' Shonna boasted, 'I'd have found out everything. About
whether they shave their heads and if they get in the bath
wearing a chemise so they can't see their own nakedness. I bet
Father Dominic is Sister Ignatious's secret lover.'

'You wouldn't have asked that in front of your mother.'

'I would so. Did he kiss you, or did your sniffling put him
off?'

Elfie saw a chance to redeem herself in Shonna's eyes. 'He
was going to kiss me, I'm sure he was. He was bending over
my bed, but the clock struck twelve and he had to go.'

Shonna laughed heartily. 'Trust you to miss out.
Cinderella!'

'But I did do quite well, didn't I?' Elfie pleaded. Shonna
jumped off the bed and surveyed herself in the mirror. 'I
suppose it will do for a start. We don't want to rush things.'

8

'The clippie's having a baby soon, a baby soon, a baby soon. It'll be born in the month of June, on a cold and fro-osty morning.'

Shonna sang at the top of her voice as she danced around the bus shelter, entertaining the queue.

'Mornings in June aren't cold and frosty. They're hot and sunny,' said Elfie, wishing that Shonna would shut up because everyone was looking at them.

Shonna took no notice and rolled up her cardigan. Stuffing it into a ball under her gym tunic, she waddled the length of the queue with her feet splayed out and her hand on the small of her back exclaiming, 'Oh my dear. My back. It does ache!'

Some of the ladies in the queue exchanged glances, smiled furtively. Margaret laughed. Shonna could be so funny, when she wanted to be, which was not often. 'How do you know? Is she showin' then?' she asked in her woman-of-the-world voice.

'She's enormous.' Shonna indicated her pouch. 'Huge. Hides it under her corsets.'

An elderly man with a white moustache leaned forward and poked her in the back with his stick. 'That's enough of that sort of talk,' he said sharply. 'There's ladies present.' Children were much too forward these days; it must be the effect of the war. Not long ago, women in a certain condition were only walked out by their husbands after dark. Now one could see whole groups of them arm in arm in the High Street, smocks stretched tight over their bulges, giggling and chattering in a most immodest fashion. They were of course evacuees, and it was probably all different in London. But they were foreigners up here, and it gave these youngsters some funny ideas.

Shonna took the cardigan from under her frock and swung it round her head, being careful to swipe him with the buttons. He flinched and rubbed his ear. The girl was a hooligan. Molly took advantage of the diversion to wander outside and sit in the gutter, in grave danger of being run over by the bus. One of the ladies hauled her inside. 'Backward kids shouldn't be let out like this. They want putting in the Homes. They're a danger to themselves and everyone else,' she remarked tartly.

'They ain't,' Margaret said. 'And she's got her rights, same as you have.' She turned to Shonna. 'How d'you know about the clippie then?'

'Aha,' said Shonna. 'That's a secret. I know what her name is. It's Nora. Nora Richards. She comes from London. She told me her fiancé's away at the front. I don't like the name Nora, it's too old-fashioned. I'll call her Nora Adora. Don't you think that's nice?'

'You said you wanted to kill her,' remembered Elfie. 'That's not very nice. I mean you shouldn't pretend to be friendly, and plot behind people's backs. My mother would say that was two-faced.'

At this turn in the conversation, there was a general sort of stiffening among the queue, a kind of tension, as they strained to hear the rest. Shonna sensed it and stared at them boldly. She liked an audience, and raised her voice. 'It's all part of my plan, getting to know her. It's like war. I'm going behind the enemy's lines. Infiltrating their defences. Then I shall strike.' Shonna looked along the queue. Their attentions seemed to be wandering. They needed a jolt.

'Of course my mother's partly to blame for this adulterating. She's a frozen woman. My father, he tells her so, often.' Heads turned back sharply in her direction. 'Of course, she can't help it. Being brought up in an orphanage as she was.'

'I thought she was the seventh child of a seventh child,' said Margaret. 'Were they all orphans?'

'Yes,' answered Shonna. 'All of them. Ill-treated and no jam when they were late for tea.' A ripple of compassion went through the queue.

'How come she met your dad then?' Margaret probed. 'You said he were very rich. Rich people don't meet orphans except in story books.'

'Oh, she left the orphanage at fourteen and went to work at the Big House.'

'She were a maid then!' exclaimed Margaret triumphantly.

'In service,' responded Shonna. 'That's different. More high-class. Lady's maids have people to wait on them. She worked for the Laird. That's Scottish for Lord, you know. It was so romantic! They fell in love and ran away. I'm a love child you know.'

'You're a liar,' said Margaret. 'And a b . . .' Shonna clapped a hand firmly over Margaret's mouth, and pinned her arm behind her back. One of the ladies said, '*Her* mouth should be washed out with soap.'

The bus arrived and the girls pushed rudely to the front of the queue and clambered on board, shoving Molly up the stairs in front of them by the seat of her pants. They flung themselves on to the back seat so that they could look down the stairwell and get a good view of the clippie. She swung out from the bus, holding the platform pole and whistling 'White Cliffs of Dover'.

Margaret looked at her reflection in the bus window. It stared back at her, thin and pinched, but quite pleased with itself. Mrs Creavy was no oil painting, and she did not seem to have done too badly, if it was all true. A laird's son, even on a bicycle, and a nice big house at the best end of the road . . . and a love child. Margaret was not too keen on getting one of those, especially if it were to turn out like Shonna. A boy would be better. It was a man's world, so you might as well have one of them. It would not be too long now before she was fourteen, and it could all start to happen. She would not go into service though. She would head for the bright lights of London, when the war was over, and the stage. Perhaps she would become a star and take over from Vera Lynn. She gave her reflection a critical look. Make-up should help.

Nora came bounding up the stairs two at a time, and Elfie looked at her stomach. The navy slacks were stretched tightly across it. It was quite flat and smooth. The corsets must be doing a good job. Nora glanced at Molly, and took a bag of sweets from her pocket. 'Have a pep?' She offered the bag of bull's eyes round, not looking directly at Shonna.

'Hello Nora,' said Shonna. The conductress looked surprised. 'I think you know my father, Mr Creavy.' Nora's face reddened. Shonna manoeuvred herself so that she was right in front of the clippie and stared her out, then she shook her head, refusing to take a sweet.

'I'll have one thank you,' said Elfie to cover her embarrassment. She took a bull's eye, popped it in her mouth and sat there, cheek bulging. Margaret followed suit, saying, 'And two halves please.'

'You needn't pay for her.' Nora indicated Molly. 'Poor little beggar.'

'Ta all the same,' said Margaret, offended. 'We've got our money.'

'Suit yourself,' replied Nora and swung off down the stairs.

'What did you say that for? You've upset her,' hissed Shonna angrily.

'Thought that's what you wanted to do,' returned Margaret. 'Make up yer mind.'

The bus reached the High Street and they ran down the stairs and jumped off. Nora had climbed up on the front bumper and was turning the handle that changed the destination. She was chatting gaily to the driver, a middle-aged woman, with shoulders like a prize fighter. As soon as they were out of earshot Margaret turned on Shonna bitterly.

'Liar! She's as flat as a board. You're having us on. I've seen me Aunty Shirley when she were in the club. I've even put me ear to her stomach and heard one of them babies ticking. Why, she's not as big as our mum.'

Shonna laughed, a nasty knowing laugh. 'Talking of your mum, how long has your dad been in Tripoli?'

Margaret thumbed her nose. 'I know what you're thinking. But it ain't true. My mum ain't up the spout. She ain't going to have any more cos our Molly went wrong.'

'Well she's a jolly funny shape.'

'I know,' said Margaret sadly. 'Slack muscles, that's what it is. When I grow up and get some money I'm going to buy her a pair of strong corsets, like that Nora's got. Then she'll be pretty and smart-looking too and you won't be able to laugh at her, Mrs Clever Dick.' Margaret scraped the shopping basket against Shonna's bare shins and turned into Liptons with her nose in the air.

'Now listen,' said Shonna, when Margaret came out again, 'and don't interrupt.' She glared at Elfie. 'We're going to call on Nora tomorrow. I've found out where she lives. There was a letter in my dad's pocket, ready to post. Looked like a birthday card. It was addressed to her.'

'You shouldn't look in people's pockets,' Elfie reminded them primly. 'It's like reading their letters. It isn't allowed.'

'It's a good job I did before my mother got there. I mean, she has to turn out his pockets when his suits go to the cleaners, doesn't she? We shall visit Nora. It'll be a surprise.'

'It'll be that all right,' said Margaret. 'She hardly knows us.'

'She knows me. I think she knows that I know about her, so she'll have to be nice to us, or else,' Shonna threatened.

Elfie knew that it was very bad manners to call unexpectedly. Her mother got quite put out by unannounced visitors, fearing they would use up the rations. She always greeted surprise callers with 'We can't give you anything to eat'. It always sounded very inhospitable to Elfie. 'Won't her mother mind?' she asked Shonna. Shonna replied that Nora had not got a mother. She lived in lodgings and was an orphan.

'Know a lot of orphans, don't you?' Margaret shifted a wad of chewing-gum to her other cheek. 'Don't you know anyone normal?'

'Another stupid remark from you and you're not coming,' said Shonna.

'Sorry I'm sure,' apologized Margaret, crossing her fingers to show Elfie she did not mean it.

'Well, keep your mouth shut,' Shonna advised. 'Nora is really refined. You don't want to parade your ignorance in front of her.'

'Pardon me for living.' Margaret pulled a face, making pretence of buttoning her lip. Elfie started to giggle.

'I just don't know why I bother with you two.' Shonna sounded really exasperated. 'You act like a pair of kids. Idiot kids at that. Well, are you coming or aren't you?'

'We're coming,' they chorused eagerly.

'She may let us try on her clothes and make-up,' Margaret whispered to Elfie. Shonna heard them. 'Whispering sends you blind,' she said tartly.

'No it don't,' Margaret countered. 'I know what do though. And I'm not telling you, see!' She ran off pulling Elfie with her, before Shonna could retaliate. When they parted Margaret told her, 'I'm going to show Shonna. I'll look real good tomorrow. I'm going to get all dressed up. It'll teach her for saying I'm common and ignorant. You wait and see.'

The next day Elfie saw Margaret waiting at the Convent gates, dank lifeless hair swept up at the sides with two clips in a poor imitation of Nora's style. Over her gymslip was an angora jumper with puff sleeves that did not fit, and which still managed to retain the full-bosomed shape of her Aunty Shirley. Margaret's skinny legs in wrinkled lisle stockings were a sickening shade of beige.

Shonna's lip curled. She walked round Margaret with slow paces, sizing her up, then held her out at arm's length, looking into her eyes. Oh dear, thought Elfie, there's going to be trouble. It'll end in a fight and we shan't go. She did not think she could bear the disappointment. Shonna was going to be cruel and show Margaret up. It was most unkind, because she only wanted to keep up with fashion and impress Nora. Margaret sensed trouble too.

'Take yer hands off me,' she warned.

To Elfie's surprise, Shonna sounded hurt. 'I only want to get a good look at you. You're really amazing. I've never seen anyone like you. Those stockings! Where did you get them?' She turned to Elfie. 'We should get ourselves some. Are they black market?'

Margaret preened herself, pulled her shoulders back and did a little twirl. 'Me Aunty Shirley got them. Queued in Woollies for hours. Weren't it kind of her to give them me?'

'Very,' returned Shonna grimly.

'Glad you like me.' Margaret tugged at a slipping stocking and secured it more firmly under the elastic band that supported it. 'I'd have liked to borrow her suspenders too, but she wouldn't lend them.'

Poor Margaret, thought Elfie. She thinks she's being admired. Shonna's very clever. It is more cruel than teasing. Shonna set off down the road and they followed in her wake, holding hands. Margaret made occasional pauses to adjust the stockings. They were led into the poorer part of the town, where they seldom ventured. The streets crowded on top of each other and the small terraced houses jostled for elbow room. A few women sat at their doorsteps with knitting and darning, enjoying a chat and the evening sunshine. They looked up as the girls clattered past on the cobbled streets, and a small child clutched at Shonna's skirt. She brushed him off like an irritating fly, and hurried on. While Margaret lagged behind extracting her heel from a grating, Shonna drew Elfie's attention to the window of a tiny house shop with assorted odds and ends in the window, pointing out a penknife right at the front.

'See that little knife. Get it.'

'What for?' asked Elfie.

'For hunting of course. On Saturday I'm taking you hunting. I'll need that knife. It's only a shilling. Don't let me down.'

They turned a corner into a really wide road, where a muddy stream ran sluggishly down a gully in the centre. The houses flanking it were large and had steps up to the front doors, with faded stripy sun-curtains. VACANCIES signs flourished beside pots of aspidistras in the windows. Shonna ran up the steps of one of the shabbier houses and rang the bell. A thin woman in a flowered crossover answered the door. 'Yes?'

'We've come to see Miss Richards,' replied Shonna.

'Are you sure?' said the landlady. 'She's not told me she's expecting anyone.'

'It's by appointment.' Shonna elbowed her way in. 'Call her please, she'll tell you she's expecting us.' While the woman was shouting up the stairs Shonna whispered to Elfie, 'Fat old cow. Who does she think she is?'

Nora came running down, just like she did on the bus, only now she was wearing a peach-coloured wrap trimmed with swansdown. Elfie thought it was the most glamorous garment she had ever seen.

Nora's slash of crimson mouth opened in surprise as she saw the girls. 'Well, hello,' she said with the slight American drawl she had picked up from visits to the army camp. 'This is a surprise. What are you lot doing here? You're a long way from home aren't you?'

Shonna was nearly as tall as Nora, and when their eyes met for a few seconds, Nora was the first to look away.

'We've come to tea,' dictated Shonna, coldly polite. 'We thought you might like some company.' Her eyes never faltered. She sounded strangely threatening. Elfie thought, if Nora throws us out, Shonna will tell her mother, I know it. Nora seemed to know it too. She hesitated, then shrugged and gave in. 'Come on up then, I'll see what I can do.' She led the way upstairs to where she lived, in the first floor front room overlooking the river.

Shonna ran to the window. 'What a lovely view. What a super room,' she exclaimed. She was acting just like an invited guest. Elfie felt dreadful. She pulled softly at Nora's robe to attract her attention. Nora looked down at her round little face. 'Please . . . we don't need tea, if you haven't got any. We don't mind at all,' she said, apologizing for Shonna's boldness. Margaret, still hovering in the doorway, caught on quickly and took her cue from Elfie. 'I don't want no tea either,' she said and patted her tummy. 'Full up. I've had all I can eat today.'

Nora's face softened. 'I think I might manage a bit of tea.' She called down to the landlady for a pot of tea and some bread and jam. Then she turned to Shonna. 'Well, we two know each other it seems. Are you going to introduce me to your friends?'

'The little one is Elfie. She's only eight. But her father's in the Government.' Shonna eyed Margaret as though she wished her to drop through the floor. 'And that . . . is . . . Margaret

. . . Groutage.' She managed to make it sound something like garbage.

Nora looked Margaret up and down. 'Well come on in then, Miss Groutage. I like a girl with a bit of style.'

Oh no, thought Elfie. Poor old Margaret; surely Nora isn't going to tease her too. She shut her eyes to blot out the thought. But Nora seemed to like what she saw, and put an arm round Margaret's shoulder. 'Make yourself at home, duck,' she welcomed.

Shonna seemed to have lost interest in Nora now that she had achieved her purpose, and gazed out of the window, lost in her own thoughts. Nora sat Elfie down on the bed and stuck an American army officer's cap on her head. 'Suits you,' she smiled. Then she looked at Margaret, who said shyly, 'I like your dressing gown.'

'You're just getting the right age to be interested in clothes,' announced Nora. She asked if Margaret would like to try on one of her sweaters, and picked out a pretty one with beads on it and handed it to her. Margaret was quite overcome and stammered out her thanks. The landlady puffed up the stairs with a tray of tea and a plate of bread and jam. Nora took it and put it on the table. 'Come on girls, tuck in then,' she told them. Elfie jumped off the bed and sat on one of the chairs. Nora added coaxingly, 'Come on Shonna,' and Shonna came away from the window reluctantly and sat with them at the table.

'Who's going to be mother?' Margaret indicated the teapot.

'Not me,' joked Nora. Elfie looked at her with round eyes. 'No. Certainly not me. The old duck wouldn't approve I'm sure.' Nora jerked her thumb in the direction of the departed landlady. Then she winked at Margaret. 'Bit old-fashioned she is. We modern gals must stick together though, mustn't we? Can't get left on the shelf. Don't want to die wondering, do we?'

'No,' said Elfie, feeling ignored. 'We don't.'

Nora reached out and put her arm round her. 'Bless the child!' she said, laughing. 'I don't think you will. You'll be a wow with the fellas one day, when you've grown up a bit.' She poured Elfie some tea and put plenty of sugar in it, then cut her bread up into small squares, really making a baby of her. Elfie was enjoying the fuss, and under Nora's protection helped herself to Shonna's share of the jam. Then, when they had finished, Nora asked Margaret if she would like to have her hair washed.

'Yes,' Shonna answered for her. 'It looks as though a wash wouldn't hurt it.'

Nora opened her mouth as if to speak, but caught Shonna's eye and shut it again. She started to pour water from the ewer to the basin, then washed and dried and brushed until Margaret's hair shone. She swept it up with a couple of combs like Loretta Young and stood back to see the effect.

'Very fetching. Just a touch of lipstick and I could take you out on the town with me.'

'Birds of a feather,' muttered Shonna. 'Come on you two. We're going.'

'But I thought you were going to keep me company.' Shonna smiled at her sweetly, but her eyes were cold. Elfie thought, she's not smiling in her heart.

'Sorry Nora, but we really must go. Elfie's only little and her mother worries so,' insisted Shonna.

'Okee dokee then,' said Nora. 'On your way.'

Elfie felt sad as she wanted to stay longer. Nora bent down and kissed her. Only then did Elfie remember that she should have looked for signs of the baby growing. She had completely forgotten. Shonna was sure to mention it on the way home. She looked desperately around for a sign of the corsets. The drawers were all open and lace-edged undies were spilling out on the floor. Nothing with whale bones at all. She had better ask before it was too late.

'Nora,' Elfie hesitated, and pointed to the chest of drawers. 'Have you . . . have you got . . . any corsets?'

Nora burst out laughing. 'Corsets? Well that's something I don't need.' She spanned her minute waist with her hands and said proudly, 'Twenty one inches.' She pointed to Shonna. 'You're fatter than I am, Shonna. You'll need corsets soon. And a brassière.' Nora looked her up and down. 'You're quite well developed, aren't you. A budding beauty.'

Shonna did not appear to be pleased. Elfie thought she might burst with rage. Nora doesn't know what she's doing, she thought, Shonna doesn't like it and we're all going to suffer on the way home.

They clattered down the stairs, Margaret still wearing the beaded sweater. As they reached the door, Nora called her back.

'Serves her right,' muttered Shonna. 'Sneaking out with a jumper.'

Margaret returned still wearing the jumper, her own in a brown paper parcel. She was clutching something else too. 'Look what she's given me.' It was a pair of very fine stockings.

Both the girls stared at her. 'Nylons!' said Elfie. Shonna seemed to have forgotten her ill humour, and fingered the gossamer material; nylons were only for Americans as yet. Then she sniffed disapprovingly. 'Told you so. She's no better than she ought to be. Goes with the Yanks. Cheap hussy.'

'I thought she was nice.' Elfie stroked the nylons gently.

'You would. You're only half sharp.'

Margaret folded the stockings carefully over her arm. 'I mustn't ladder them. Aunty'll have to lend her suspenders now.'

'Why?' asked Shonna coldly.

'So's I can keep them up of course.'

'Don't bother. You're not going to wear them. They're mine, see!'

'They are not,' said Elfie indignantly. 'They're Margaret's. Nora gave them to her.'

'Ah, I took you there, didn't I? Any spoils from the visit are mine. But I don't like the sweater.' Shonna started tugging at the nylons, but Margaret held fast. Shonna pulled harder. The stockings stretched out between them, long and transparent.

'Don't tear them,' Margaret pleaded.

'I will, unless you hand them over.'

For one terrible moment Elfie could see the nylons being ripped in two. How could anyone be so spiteful to something so lovely, after Nora had been so generous? Nora was kind and had seen that Margaret was trying hard to look good, without much to go on. The two girls were now facing each other, ugly with determination and spite, the nylons thin as a rope taut between them. Then Margaret suddenly let go. The stockings snapped back to Shonna who nearly overbalanced.

'Have them,' Margaret shouted. 'And bad luck to you.'

She ran off, her shoulders shaking with sobs. Elfie followed her, not caring for once what Shonna thought. She shouted after them, 'Cry Baby cry-y.' They turned at the corner and looked back just in time to see her tie the nylons in a knot and post them in a letter-box.

Margaret rapped on the window pane to stop Molly cutting up worms with a stone, and then took the kettle from the stove and poured boiling water into the big brown teapot. 'Sit down,' she told Elfie, and started to pour the tea. Mrs Groutage had gone to see Stewart Granger; she never missed a matinée.

'Two spoonfuls please,' said Elfie.

'You should cut it out,' said Margaret. 'It is wartime and Shonna's right, you're getting too fat.' She put one spoonful into the cup, then seeing Elfie's lip drooping, relented and added another. 'She's not going to get away with it,' Margaret went on. 'It's not as though she wanted them nylons for herself. Dog in the manger . . . that's her. I'm going to punish her. See if I don't.'

'What will you do?'

'Play her at her own game. That's what. Put one of her own bleeding spells on her. I'm better at it than her anyway. Remember the Plasticine man. Put the mockers on him all right, didn't I? Her dad had three weeks in hospital.'

'I know,' said Elfie. 'But he still sees Nora, doesn't he?'

'Well I didn't get it quite right. But if it works a bit I'll be happy.' Margaret's face tensed. 'She's a thief. That's what she is. Her hands should be cut off like it says in the Bible.'

'It doesn't,' said Elfie. 'Not in my Bible.'

'Yours is a Catholic Bible, that's different.' Margaret opened a drawer in the sideboard and took out a little parcel wrapped in newspaper. 'Look,' she said, opening it.

'What's that?' Elfie looked at the strange little straw figure that was revealed. It wore both skirt and trousers and did not have any features on its face.

'It's a fatility doll. Used for old fatility rites. It belonged to my granny. She was a countrywoman.' Margaret was almost as good as Shonna with tales of her relatives. Elfie sometimes wondered why her own folk were all so dull. She supposed it must be because they came from Wisbech. 'What does it do?' she asked.

'It's called a corn dolly. Made from the first corn of the harvest,' Margaret explained. 'It's got strong magic powers. I'll do better with this than with the Plasticine man. You'll see. I'm going to bury it in a horrible grave. I'll tie its hands up. When it rots, and I reckon that'll take about three months, her thieving hands will drop off. Serves her right too.'

'Yes,' agreed Elfie. 'She should be punished. But she does make the games fun, doesn't she? It's not so exciting without her.'

'That's your trouble,' Margaret retorted. 'You're always hankering after her. Gives her a big head. No one else bothers with her. You'd better start doing wivout her cos if my spell works you'll be looking for a new friend.'

'I'm not sure I want to do it,' said Elfie. 'Look, couldn't we just tell Nora secretly. She'd understand. I know she would. Perhaps she'd give you another pair.'

'And perhaps not. Grown-ups can't be trusted to do what you want. I reckon she was a bit scared of Shonna anyway. Guessed what a rotten little sneak she is. She'd be careful not to upset her now, wouldn't she? Because of Shonna telling her mum. She's not only a thief but a blackmailer too.'

'I suppose so,' said Elfie. She did not know what blackmail was, but there was no denying Shonna was a sneak.

Margaret rapped on the window pane again to call Molly in, and helped her on with her coat. 'Drink up your tea,' she told Elfie, 'and let's get going.'

Margaret took them to the disused churchyard in the old part of the town, where the graves were so lichen-covered that most of the names were unreadable. She stopped in front of a big square one with writing on both sides. 'This is it,' she announced.

'I thought you said a horrible grave,' said Elfie. 'This one's not really horrible. You can even read the writing.'

'Yes, and if you read it you'll find out why it's so horrible. There's seven people in here. That's why it's a big'un. Seven. All in one family. Wiped out in the plague.'

Elfie looked at the stone. Molly was busy trying to climb up it. Thomas ffirman . . . That was funny, to have your name start with two ffs. Buried with his wife Anna, or was it Hanna? She could not see for a patch of lichen. Then all the little children underneath, Susanna, Mary, Thomas, Amy and William. He must have been the baby. He'd been born and died in the same week. That was really sad. Margaret shouldn't be digging in graves, it wasn't nice. Molly was sitting on it now and sifting the little mounds of earth that sat on top. The place had a quiet, eerie feel about it. One of the little mounds started to move. Elfie clutched at Margaret's sleeve. 'Look! What's that?'

Margaret laughed. 'Don't worry, it's not them trying to get out. It's only molehills, that's what.' She started to scrabble in the earth, scooping out a hole. When it was deep enough, she pushed the corn dolly into it, its wrists tied up with red wool, and smoothed the soil back. Then Margaret recited, 'Amen ever and ever for glory and power the kingdom is Thine.' She stood up, looking satisfied. 'There! That'll do.'

'Was that a spell?' Elfie was doubtful.

'It were the Lord's Prayer backwards. Leastways it was some of it. You don't need very much. It's quite powerful.'

'Is this a secret?' asked Elfie.

'Course it is. You know and I know, and that's all. Molly don't understand. When Shonna's hands start to rot she'll wonder what's happening. Then we'll tell her and she'll be sorry. She might even get me some more nylons to take the spell off.'

They wandered round the old churchyard looking at a few more graves and picking some weeds to make into a bunch of flowers for Molly. Lots of the graves had RIP at the ends of the names.

'Why do they keep putting RIP on them?' Margaret asked. Elfie replied that they were Catholic graves, and it meant rest in peace, which was nice.

'Shonna'll never rest in peace in hers, cos I've wished it on her.'

'You shouldn't do that,' said the shocked Elfie, 'it's very wicked. You should write something nice on graves like "Sleeping where no shadows fall". Little June's got "Who plucked this flower" on hers.'

'Who what?' Margaret's brow wrinkled.

'"Who plucked this flower? I did, the Master said, and the gardener was silent." Don't you think that's lovely?'

'No I don't. You might as well have "Who killed Cock Robin", and be done with it.'

'Oh,' said Elfie and bit her lip hard. She changed the subject quickly in case she cried. 'I wish the spell would work at once. Can't you hurry it up a bit. It would be nice if you could have the nylons for Sunday.'

'No,' Margaret said. 'It can't be hurried. My granny always said the mills of God grind slowly. We shall have to wait and see.' She walked them home the long way so they could pass Jimmy Day's house. He was cleaning out his rabbit hutch by the front porch. When he saw them he looked the other way and started whistling.

'Why is he pretending not to see us?' Elfie asked.

'Who?'

'Jimmy of course.'

'Who's Jimmy?' Margaret hurried past, her cheeks glowing. 'I don't know any Jimmies.'

If Margaret could really do spells, why didn't she do one on Jimmy. Make him grow tall and handsome, or turn him into Tyrone Power. Perhaps Shonna could do it, if of course Margaret's spell did not work, and she survived.

9

On Friday after school Elfie found her way back to the streets
of little houses. A group of children hopscotched on the
cracked pavement using a chalky stone to mark the squares.
It scraped on the concrete setting Elfie's teeth on edge as she
tried to sidle past. She knew that she was off her own territory
and hoped they would carry on with the game and ignore her.
She stepped out into the gutter to avoid them, but as she
passed a short tow-headed chap barred her way. 'Stop! You
ain't coming down here.'

Elfie tried to back away but a rough-looking girl caught
hold of her by the arm and twisted it in a Chinese burn.
'What's yer name?'

'Elfreda. Elfreda Brown. I'm usually called Elfie.'

'Then what you doing down here? That's a posh name
and you look like one of them posh kids. Are you a posh kid?
Are you from that Convent up town?' She twisted the arm
harder.

'Leave me alone!' Elfie cried.

'Where d'you think you're going eh?'

Elfie looked at her assailant. Her hair hung in greasy tangles
and her mouth was covered in scabs, dabbed with purple.
Purple. It could be catching. She remembered the worms that

Shonna had told her about, and made a desperate effort, freeing herself of the girl's hands.

'I'm only going to the shop,' she whimpered.

'Got money?'

'No,' said Elfie truthfully.

'Liar.' The girl grabbed the purse that hung round her neck and jerked it, breaking the strap. She opened it and looked inside.

'There's nowt in it,' she commented accusingly.

'No. I only had my dinner money.' Elfie was glad now that she had tucked the postal order into her knicker pocket. The big girl would not think to look there. Her knickers would not have any pockets. Only expensive knickers had pockets. The ones from Sanders the Outfitters in the High Street. The girl got hold of Elfie's gasmask strap and twisted it round and round, threatening to strangle her.

'There ain't no shop here, anyway.' She turned to the group of children. 'Ain't no shop here, is there?'

'We ain't got a sho-op, we ain't got a shop,' they sing-songed. Then as though at a secret signal they surrounded her, and the big girl gathered a globule of spit in her mouth and gobbed it at Elfie's face. Elfie jumped aside and it landed on her blazer sleeve. The purse went spinning over her head into the gutter. Her eyes were smarting with tears. What would her mother say? Little ladies did not go home with spit on their clothes and their purses torn. She would be in terrible trouble. She sniffed loudly. The children danced round her singing 'Poor Jenny sits a-weeping on a bright summer's day'. Elfie ran round the circle trying to find a way out, but they pushed her from one to the other, calling 'pig face' and 'snotty nose', until one of them broke the circle and let her through. She retrieved her purse and ran down the street, stopping at last in front of the shop. Of course there was a shop. They had been teasing her. It was still there and the little tortoiseshell knife was in exactly the same place. Thank goodness it had not gone.

Everyone in the world must want a pretty knife like that. Not to get it would mean that Shonna would not take her hunting tomorrow, like she had promised. Elfie hesitated in the doorway trying to pluck up the courage to go in.

She had never bought anything except a lolly in a shop before, but Margaret shopped for her mother every week; went to the Co-op like a grown-up lady and handed a list to the assistant. She sat up at the counter on a high stool while the lady packed the goods in a basket. Elfie stood beside her inhaling the lovely pungent odours of bacon and cheese. Then Margaret would hand over the money. Two whole pound notes. The assistant placed them in a sort of wooden tennis ball and sent it hurtling round the shop on a set of overhead tramlines. When it came creaking back, the assistant pulled it down and opened it, and there was Margaret's change. Elfie thought that when she grew up she might like to work in a grocery shop. It would have to be the 'Home and Colonial' of course, or her mother would not approve. The 'Home and Colonial' did not take money. You had an account and the errand boy trundled your order home on a bicycle with a big basket in front. The 'Home and Colonial' certainly would not have the tennis balls. She must tell her mother how nice it was at the Co-op.

A fat woman pushed past her, breaking into her dreams. She left a sourish smell in her wake. Elfie plucked up courage and followed her in. The shop was dark inside, but she could just make out a diminutive man standing behind a makeshift counter. As she got closer she could see brown stains on his moustache and some egg down his waistcoat. He was lucky to get a fresh egg these days.

The woman took out a piece of paper from her purse and pushed it across the counter. She's paying with a postal order like me, Elfie thought. He looked at it and went to the back of the shop, returning with a man's suit over his arm. The woman slapped three shilling pieces on the counter.

Oh dear, thought Elfie. She's giving him money as well. The lady turned to go. 'See you Monday as usual,' she told him.

Now it was Elfie's turn. 'Yes, young Miss?'

'Please Sir, I'd like the little knife at the front of the window. The tortoiseshell one.'

He slid back a glass panel and reached for the knife. 'That'll be a shilling.'

'Please Sir, I haven't any money . . .' He dropped the knife back into the window. 'But I've got a postal order.'

'Let's have a look then.'

Elfie had to fumble in her knicker pocket. He did not look the other way. What a rude man. She handed the postal order over, a bit the worse for wear. He held it up to the light as though it was a £5 note. 'Not pinched it have you?'

'No sir. It's from my Auntie Mabel. She lives in Wisbech. She sends me one every year, for my birthday.' He grunted and stuck it in his waistcoat pocket, handing her the knife in exchange. 'Careful, it's sharp,' he warned her. Elfie left the shop, putting the knife in her pocket. The street children had disappeared now, and she ran home quickly.

Ignoring her mother's shouts of 'Elfie! Tea's ready', she raced up the stairs to her room. The knife was the most exciting thing she had ever owned. The blade came out on a spring, sharp and shiny. Shonna would be very pleased.

It might be a good idea to try the knife out on something. One of Elfie's plaits was hanging over her shoulder, and she held it in her left hand and sliced gently. The end, just below the bow, came away in her hand. The knife could be dangerous. The man was right to warn her. She looked at herself in the mirror. Her mother was going to notice and be cross. She loosened the plait and did it up again, tighter this time. Now she had one fat plait and one thin one, but they were both the same length, well, almost. She wished the knife was to have a nicer purpose than hunting, but the Scottish were very fond of it as a pastime, weren't they? Didn't they sing at school:

> 'My heart's in the Highlands, my heart is not here.
> My heart's in the Highlands, a-chasing the deer.'

Elfie was sure that she had seen Shonna's eyes become misty with tears when they sang it. She must be pining. And while there may not be any deer on the fenlands, there might be a rabbit or two, or even a little squirrel. Something she could catch and bring home for a pet. She hoped the knife was to cut twigs for a lair because she had not liked the sight of blood since Shonna had pricked their fingers, and she did not want to be a nurse any more. It would be nice to live with a rabbit and a squirrel and be like little Josie in the comic, who lived with a rabbit and a mouse and called the rabbit 'Bun'.

Downstairs her mother looked at her and cocked her head to one side. Then she tilted it the other way. Then she got hold of Elfie's head and tipped it first one way, then the other. She frowned. 'Funny, I could have sworn one of your plaits looked shorter than the other.'

Saturday dawned blustery and threatening rain. Wispy grey clouds scudded across the sky like dirty foam and the March winds flattened the grass to a silvery sheen. Elfie did not care about the weather, for today was the hunting day. And more important, it was her ninth birthday too. Jumping the last three steps she swung round the newel post in excitement.

'Mind the paintwork,' shouted her mother, who was washing up at the kitchen sink. 'Happy birthday dear.' She wiped her hands on the teatowel and kissed Elfie on the cheek, pointing to the table where two parcels lay with some envelopes beside her porridge bowl.

Elfie opened the cards first so as not to look greedy. After all, it was the wishes that counted most, was it not? There was one from Shonna with an outsize NINE embossed in gold leaf, and one from her parents of a girl in a crinoline outside a cottage. Margaret had sent a home-made job, printing HAPPY BERTHDAY ELF in capitals. The shaky crosses must have been added by Molly. Elfie smiled and showed them to her mother, who put her glasses on and looked, remarking that Shonna's card was perhaps a bit showy, but typical of that family, and should not Margaret be spelling correctly now that she was at the senior school?

Elfie opened the parcels. The big one, from her parents, contained a shop-bought dress, the first one she had ever owned. Every day on the way to school she had admired it on the shop window dummy, not daring to hope it would ever be hers. Made of Prince of Wales check, it was pleated all round the skirt; very grown-up and smart. She ran to try it on in front of the hall mirror, fumbling with the buttons in her haste to see herself in it. Was that really her? How disappointing. I should be tall and slim for a dress like this, she thought, and Shirley Temple curls would look better than plaits. She pulled her tummy in. That was better. She must refuse second helpings of pudding. Her mother, coming out to look, frowned. 'It's a bit tight in the wrong places, but perhaps you'll slim down as you grow dear.'

In the smaller parcel was a beautiful velvet box lined with white satin. Nestling in this, a locket on a fine gold chain. From her godmother in London, it was delicate and expensive-looking. Her mother sighed when she saw it, 'It's so easy to have good taste when you've got money.' Mrs Brown started rummaging on the mantelpiece. She is looking for the postal order, thought Elfie. I hope she does not give me the shilling instead. If I took it, I would be cheating. It might even be stealing. I would have to own up. She sat there holding her breath while her mother moved letters and bills along the dusty surface, saying that she was sure she had put it there, it must have blown off. Then she abandoned the search, put on her hat with the veiling, and started wrapping a bunch of flowers.

Oh gosh, thought Elfie, it's cemetery day. The excitement had made her forget. Oh surely we're not going today, on my birthday. Shonna will call while I'm out and she'll go hunting without me. I shall have to say something.

'Please Mummy . . . I don't want to go today. It is my birthday.'

Her mother's face looked ugly, contorted with suppressed grief. 'June never even had a birthday,' she said, in a tight, choked voice.

Elfie quickly put on her coat. 'I didn't mean it, really I didn't. I will come.' June was still part of the family and it meant a lot to Mummy that they visited her today so that she could share the birthday too. They set out in silence for the bus.

Everything seemed to be in slow motion. The bus queues were longer and the passengers older. They took such a time to embark, clutching the rails feebly and tottering to their seats. The conductress – it wasn't Nora – waited till the last one was settled before ringing the bell. Even when they reached the cemetery her mother kept stopping to talk to people, men with black armbands and sad-faced ladies. Elfie looked for a watering can to help her mother and discovered a family of beetles behind one of the headstones. Stooping to watch their endeavours, she forgot the can and became thoroughly engrossed in the insect life. Her mother, tired of waiting, carried the vase to the water tank herself. She arranged the flowers prettily, then stood by the little cross fingering her rosary. A passing family averted their eyes from the sad scene.

At last, after what seemed a lifetime to Elfie, they were back at home. She had no way of knowing if Shonna had already called, and passed the time cutting snaps from the family album, one of herself and one of June, to put in the locket.

They should stay there forever, and nobody was ever going to be allowed to take them out.

Later in the afternoon Shonna appeared at the gate, a check bundle slung Dick Whittington style over her shoulder. That'll be her tea, Elfie thought. She asked her mother for some but Mrs Brown said she did not pack meals. She was not a seaside landlady, and added that Elfie's tea would be on the table at the usual time. If she did not come in to eat it she must go without.

Elfie snatched a bit of bread and marge off the kitchen table as she ran out, and stuffed it in her coat pocket. This'll tide me over, she thought, and if I don't fancy it, I'll give it to the rabbit on the way back. Her mother called after her, 'Don't be late for tea. Remember it's your birthday.'

'Hello birthday girl.' Shonna looked down to where the hem of Elfie's new dress was hanging below her coat. 'What's that you've got on?'

'It's my birthday frock. It's a real shop-bought one.'

Shonna's eyes narrowed. 'Your mother's got awful taste. No flair at all. Now my mother's got real flair. Got it from Her Ladyship at the Big House. All *her* clothes came from Paris. France.'

Mrs Creavy wandered into Elfie's mind in her pinny, a hedgehog of pins in her hair. Better not to argue with Shonna though, in case she called the trip off. Elfie showed her the locket proudly, opening it to display the photos.

'Better give that to me to look after. You're bound to lose it.'

'But I want to wear it. It's a birthday present.'

'Well, lose it then. See if I care.' Shonna looked as though she was going to sulk.

'Take it,' said Elfie, turning her back so that Shonna could unloose the locket from her neck. 'But be careful with it.' They set off in the direction of the town. Elfie pulled at

Shonna's sleeve. 'We're going the wrong way . . . for hunting I mean.'

Shonna stopped abruptly and faced her. 'That's what you think,' she said. Then she set off again at such a brisk pace that Elfie had to run to keep up with her. They had only got as far as the library when Shonna said she was going to eat her tea. She sat down on a bench and started to spread out her picnic.

'Shouldn't we be sitting in a field, eating our sandwiches, while the cows and sheep chew the cud and watch us?'

Shonna, her cheeks bulging with bread and ham, replied that sheep did not chew cud, and then ate her way through the sandwiches and a slice of fruit cake. She did not offer any to Elfie, who looked on, mouth watering. She did not dare bring out her bread and margarine, and felt embarrassed to watch Shonna tucking in in full view of the Saturday shoppers. Shonna finished her food, rolled up the check napkin, and threw it into the gutter as though it was a paper party one. They set off once again, this time for the bus station. That's better, thought Elfie, we're going to catch a bus and ride into the country. I wonder if they will let me bring the rabbit back on it? Perhaps he could travel half fare. Anyway, Shonna always has some money and if Nora is on the bus we might not even have to pay. Then Shonna grabbed her, pinching her arm.

'Quick,' she said, pulling Elfie into a telephone box. 'In here. Put your gasmask on.'

Was there a raid? The siren had not gone. Elfie struggled into her mask. It was the Mickey Mouse one she had refused to give up for the regulation black that Shonna was putting on. It smelled stuffy, of warm rubber. She had only worn it once before, in an air raid drill at school.

They peered out through the smudged glass, not seeing very much. Shonna took out her hanky and rubbed at the panes so they could see better. A few passengers saw them and grinned. Children could be so funny. A straggly queue of people formed outside the booth, stamping and coughing impatiently. Shonna kept putting money in the box, then pressing button 'B' to get it back. She drew Elfie's attention to a number five bus, just drawing in. The quarry was on board.

They watched as she put her ticket machine away in the platform cupboard, picked up her bag and made for the station office, emerging minutes later, a chrysalis transformed. A poppy-covered dress replaced the navy slacks, and a costume jacket was slung casually over her shoulders. Nora's shapely calves were set off by wedge-heeled shoes strapped around the ankles. She made for the entrance and hovered there, looking anxiously up and down the road.

They continued to watch her from their hiding place until an angry man pulled them out. They ran and flattened themselves against the wall, poking the snouts of the masks round the corner as they peeped out. A tall dark figure appeared and took Nora into his arms, bending his head to reveal a bald patch. Mr Creavy! And without his Homburg. He had made no other concession to casual clothing and was wearing his dark jacket and pinstripes. He must have come from work. Nora Adora leaned her head against his lapels, and he stroked her hair tenderly.

Elfie got quite carried away under her gasmask, charmed by the romance. It would have been even better if Nora had been meeting an American Officer. But Mr Creavy would have to do for now, even if he was not such a heart-throb. Shonna was jumping about excitedly. It was impossible to know what she was thinking under the mask, but she could not be surprised; she must have known Nora would be on that bus. The couple linked arms and set off from the bus station. Shonna indicated that they were to follow. She hissed, 'Did you bring the knife?'

Elfie nodded reluctantly. Stalking Nora and Mr Creavy with

a knife was not going to be much fun. She wished she had said no. Whatever was Shonna going to do? They started tracking the couple, keeping close. They dodged in and out of shop doorways, and hid behind pillar-boxes and bus shelters. Elfie's view was very restricted because the mask hampered her movements. She could only see bottoms, mostly funny ones, fat wobblers that cut out the light and tight corseted ones with no division. How did they sit down? Nora's was cute and wiggled as she walked. It seemed to have a life of its own. Mr Creavy was bottomless. His legs went on forever like a giraffe's.

Right through the town and out towards Wicken Fen. There were no shop doorways to protect them now and the tracking was getting really exciting. Elfie's mask steamed up completely and she pulled it off, gulping in the fresh air. Shonna had taken hers off too, and had pulled her scarf over her mouth, bandit style.

The few trees out in the open were twisted and stunted, but grasses and sage grew almost knee high. They dropped on to their stomachs and crawled, Red Indian style. They must not be seen. It was such fun that Elfie forgot about the rabbit. After a while they tired, their breath coming out like puffs from a steam engine. Resting behind a bush they could see the couple in the distance. Silhouettes, holding hands like paper cut-outs. Nora pointed to her shoe, she seemed to be having difficulties. Mr Creavy swung her up in his arms and carried her like a child. Where were they going?

A group of land-girls in an adjacent field were digging potatoes. Shonna ran over and asked one of them the time. The woman stopped, and leaned forward, resting her heavy bosom upon the handle of her spade while she consulted a man's watch. It was twenty past four. 'Why did you do that?' Elfie asked. 'You have a watch of your own.'

Shonna replied that all land-girls liked to be asked the time, it gave them an excuse to stop work. She must be right as they had all given up now and were staring in the direction of the blackened old windmill by the river, where Mr Creavy was heading, still carrying Nora. The fat one with the watch bent her arm up and made a fist, thumping her elbow with her other hand. The rest of the land-girls roared with laughter. They were not very ladylike and Elfie thought she would not like to be one when she grew up, even to help the war effort. Shonna said, 'Come on. Don't loiter,' and pulled her back in the direction they had just come from.

'Why are we going back?'

'We're not. But I don't want *them* to see where we're going. They can't be trusted to mind their own business.' She pointed in the direction of the land-girls, then pulled Elfie to the ground, and they crawled on their stomachs again in the direction of the mill until they were safely past them. When they reached the mill Shonna hauled Elfie to her feet, insisting, 'Keep quiet now, and give me the knife.'

Elfie said nothing and tightened her grip on it. What if Shonna really meant to kill Nora and it was not just a game? She could burn in hell for that. She imagined herself impaled on a fork, struggling and shouting as the Devil pitched her into the flames. She was not too sure, either, if children could be hanged for murder.

Shonna wasted no time arguing and delved into Elfie's pocket. A silent struggle ensued. Prizing her fingers off the knife with her nails, Shonna held it aloft in triumph then sliced the head off a thistle to test the blade. Elfie watched her, terrified. But all Shonna did was go up to the mill and plunge the knife into a knothole level with her eye. Then she twisted it round till she had gouged out a core from the rotten timber. She stuck her finger in it to test its patency and knelt down to make another one below, indicating to Elfie to put her eye to it.

At first Elfie could see nothing, but then she became accustomed to the hazy light that filtered from the window high up on the wall. Because of the angle of the knothole she could only make out Mr Creavy's long striped legs next to Nora's pale slim ones. Nora had kicked off the troublesome shoes now, and her toes curled downwards and gripped the sandy floor, and wriggled. Elfie hoped she had not got blisters.

While she watched, Mr Creavy's trousers dropped to the floor, and stayed there, pooled around his ankles. His braces must have broken. Elfie wondered if he carried a safety-pin for emergencies, like she did. Now his legs had started to make rhythmic movements. Surely he would not be dancing because it was a funny place to do it. Could he perhaps be doing PT? He should pull his trousers up first. Anyway, whatever it was, Nora was doing it with him now, and that was fun.

'Up and down, up and down, all the way to London
   town,' Elfie mouthed,
'Crisscross crisscross all the way to King's Cross
Knees bend, knees bend, all the way to Land's End.'

It must be fun to have a father like Mr Creavy. Her own would be asleep in the armchair by now with a hanky over his face. People should not have children when they were so old. It was not fair. She looked up at Shonna to see what she was doing, but Shonna's eye was fixed firmly to her own spyhole. Her other one was screwed up tightly and her mouth had dropped open. She did not look pretty now, Elfie thought with satisfaction, and made up her mind to always keep her chin up and her lips pressed firmly together. There was something about her concentration, though, that made Elfie look back again into the mill.

Mr Creavy had kicked the trousers off altogether now and his feet were jerking forward in little spasms. His legs looked so funny with just his socks and shoes on. He was very naughty; you should not take your clothes off in front of people, however well you knew them.

Suddenly Shonna grabbed Elfie and pulled her towards the ditch. She pushed her down till her face was close to the brackish water and held her there for a long time. When Shonna let her get up again, Mr Creavy and Nora were walking back across the fields, arms around each other. Nora was tripping along barefoot on the grass and laughing. He was carrying her shoes. As the rain came pattering down, they started to run and Elfie could feel their happiness within her. She was glad that Nora was not cross with him for taking his trousers off.

Now Elfie looked down at herself. What a sorry sight! Her new dress had trailed in the water, and her coat was caked with mud. She dripped steadily on to the grass, her shoes squelching. Shonna remained quite neat. Hardly a hair out of place.

'I'll be in trouble when I get home,' Elfie wailed. 'Just look at me!'

'Don't whine. It was worth it, wasn't it?'

'No. My new dress is spoiled and we didn't get a rabbit.'

'A rabbit! Who wants a rabbit?' Shonna said tersely and started to walk home.

Elfie followed her, still complaining, 'You said we were going hunting, Shonna. Really you did. You promised me a rabbit, well almost promised.'

Shonna turned round, took hold of her by the shoulders and shook her hard. 'Shut up! That's enough. I'm fed up with you. I take you to see something really exciting and all you do is bleat about a rabbit. For God's sake go and find someone of your own age to play with if all you want is a rabbit.'

'It wasn't exciting. It was rude,' said Elfie. 'Your father took his trousers off. So there.'

Shonna laughed. 'That's not rude. Not when grown-ups do it. That's what they all do when they get together. They call it sexual intercourse. It's how they make babies. They take all their clothes off and jump about on top of each other.'

Elfie looked at her wide-eyed. 'They don't, do they? Why were your dad and Nora standing up, if that's what whey were doing?'

'He wouldn't want her to get sand on her bottom would he? Anyway you can do it standing up, or sitting down or like a wheelbarrow. I've seen this picture from an Indian temple. Douglas Ingram was showing it to the girls on the hockey pitch. Maureen Gatesby went crying off home to her mum, the rotten sneak. We'll probably all cop it now. When I grow up I might marry an Indian. They seem to know a lot about it.'

'It doesn't sound nice. I don't think Mummy and Daddy would do it.'

'Course they do. How do you think they got you, and June. You listen at night, when everything's quiet. The bed springs will start to creak. I bet your old folk are really polite about it all. I bet he says "Excuse me dear" as he pulls her nightie up. I bet he does it with his pipe in his mouth.' Shonna sniggered.

'I don't believe you.'

'Don't. But I've tried my best to educate you. Don't blame me if you grow up ignorant. You'll have to do it yourself one day. Really. Ask Margaret if you don't believe me. I reckon she's doing it already cos she smokes. You can tell by their eyes if they have. Her voice is more serious. I have to find out if they enjoy it, before I have a go.' Shonna thought for a moment and then said, 'They do.'

When they reached the garden gate Elfie asked for her locket back. Shonna fumbled in her blazer pocket and pulled a face. 'I've lost it. Don't cry. I'll get you another.' She shoved Elfie in the gate.

The light was on in the dining room, her parents must be

in there. She could hear the Ovaltinees on the wireless, so it was six o'clock. She was very late. Quietly pushing open the door she was surprised by the festive sight. The table was set with the best crocheted cloth. In the middle was a pink iced cake with nine candles. Side by side with a plate of chocolate biscuits, some dainty sandwiches marked the passage of time by curling at the edges. Her father sat by the fire smoking his pipe and listening to the programme. He looked up and saw her standing there.

'Where on earth have you been? I was beginning to get worried.' He caught sight of her clothes. 'You're caked in mud. You look as if you've been dragged through a field. Whatever's happened to you?' Without waiting for an answer he helped her off with her coat. 'We'll leave it to dry and brush the mud off before mother sees it. She'd have a fit.'

'Where is she?' Elfie asked.

'Gone to bed. She was a bit upset. Doesn't like you out with that girl, you know. Left you a note.'

Elfie took the folded slip of paper and opened it. 'How could you? On your birthday too. Don't come and look for me. I don't want to see you.'

'I'm sorry,' she sobbed. 'I forgot. I was only playing with Shonna. I didn't know the time.'

'Never mind duck,' said her father kindly. He looked at her, then at the note. Doris was getting awfully sharp lately. He supposed she was still fretting for the baby. She did not seem to have any patience with Elfie.

'I'll have tea with you,' he volunteered, sitting down and putting a party hat on his head. It was a purple crown and did not go at all well with his droopy moustache. He looked funny, and sad at the same time. Elfie burst into tears again. They were her family, her Mummy and Daddy, and she shouldn't upset them so. Why hadn't she remembered? It was very selfish of her when they had prepared a lovely surprise and sat all afternoon waiting for her to come home. She sniffed loudly and tried to eat a piece of cake, but it stuck in her throat and she choked.

Her father got up and patted her on the back. 'Choke up chicken,' he said. 'Come on, don't take on so. I don't mind you playing with your friend. You're only a child once.' He sighed. 'Have some fun while you're young and innocent.'

Shonna's attitude to Elfie had undergone a change. Since the day at the mill she did not seek her company any more, and even tried to avoid her. I just don't know what I've done, thought Elfie. Perhaps she's avoiding me because of the locket. I could tell her it doesn't matter, but it does. If my mother asks where it is I will be in real trouble.

Shonna seemed to have forgotten her promise about getting a new one. Elfie posted a note through Shonna's door, 'Please get me a locket before my mother finds out. *Please* Shonna. Love Elfie.'

The next day, Shonna called at her house and took a twist of tissue paper out of her pocket. She gave it to Elfie. 'Here you are,' she said. 'You can stop whittling.'

Elfie undid the paper and found a locket, that looked exactly like the one she had lost. 'Oh Shonna! You must have spent all your money.'

'It was only a cheap one,' Shonna replied. 'The kind of rubbish your relatives always buy.'

Elfie was too delighted to see it to be hurt. Now her mother need never know. Shonna had been clever to find one like it. She must have a good memory as she had hardly seemed to look at it at the time. Of course, the photos were missing and that was sad, because the picture of June was the only one in the album. Still, her mother had a big portrait of June over the mantelpiece with flowers under it, so perhaps she would not miss it. Elfie asked Shonna to fasten the locket round her neck.

'Will you play?' she asked.

'Later,' said Shonna, and ran off after some older girls who were passing, leaving Elfie alone with the locket.

Elfie rapped on the letterbox of Margaret's house and Mrs Groutage came to the door in her petticoat, looking sleepy. She had pulled a cardigan round her shoulders, as if she had just got up. Behind her in the scullery Elfie could see Molly tied on to the kitchen chair with Tom's football scarf, a plate of bread and jam in front of her. She was eating her way steadily through it. A man's voice shouted from upstairs: 'Come on Edie, hurry it up!'

Mrs Groutage spoke a bit sharply. Margaret was out, she said. Didn't Elfie know she had a fella now. Been walking out with him for a couple of weeks. A bit young perhaps, but we all have to start somewhere don't we? Perhaps Elfie should find a little friend of her own age. Would she like to play with Molly? She turned and pointed to the dribbling youngster. Elfie's refusal came a bit too quickly, and Mrs Groutage took offence and went in, giving the door a slam that made the glass rattle. Miserably Elfie wandered off to the park in search of Jimmy and Margaret. Perhaps if she told them how lonely she was, they would take pity on her and play with her for a while, or at least let her sit with them and listen to them talk. There were plenty of children playing in the park now the nights were getting lighter. A group of girls started skipping to a rhyme, twirling the rope and jumping in and out, having fun.

'Vote vote vote for good old Hitler,
Calling Mary at the door.
Fo-or Mary is the one, and we'll have some jolly fun.
And we won't vote for Hitler any more.'

As the next girl jumped into the rope, the previous one ran off. Trip and you were out. Elfie stood in the crowd. Perhaps someone would call her name. But nobody did, and after a while she realized it was because no one knew her. They were not Convent girls. She wandered away and in the distance saw Jimmy and Margaret making for the bandstand. She followed them slowly and mounted the steps, looking down through the wrought-iron grids to the litter below. People were very untidy, and in spite of the sweet rationing there were lots of toffee papers.

By the time Elfie reached the top step Margaret, as predicted by her mother, was making a start, lying full length on the bench that encircled the stand. Jimmy Day, now promoted to long trousers, lay on top of her. One of her hands was ruffling his crest of hair, the other drooped towards the floor . . . holding a cigarette.

Gosh and golly, Elfie thought admiringly, she is daring. And it looks as if they are French kissing. The kiss was a long one and Elfie stood watching as it went on and on. Then she coughed politely to let them know she was there. Margaret, her privacy invaded, threw Jimmy off, drawing up her knees to reveal a pair of borrowed pink camiknickers. She sat up, her mouth looking as if it had been smeared with jam. Elfie immediately recognized the colour of Mrs Groutage's lipstick. Margaret looked annoyed.

'Phew! You didn't half give me a scare. I thought it was the parkie. What d'you want?'

'Nothing, I was just having a walk. I saw you.'

'Well, run off home then,' said Margaret. 'It's nearly supper-time. Your mum'll be wondering where you are.'

'I thought perhaps I could stop with you for a bit,' Elfie begged.

Margaret caught the tone of her voice. 'Look, I'll play with you tomorrow. Promise, scout's honour.' She put two fingers up in mock salute.

'You're not a scout, you're not even a girl guide. Anyway tomorrow's Sunday and I have to go to Mass in the morning and Sunday school in the afternoon,' Elfie added miserably. 'I want someone to play with now.'

'Look Elf. Buzz off. There's a good kid. I'll come out with you on Monday. Promise. When Jim's at football.'

Hearing his name mentioned, Jimmy started to take an interest in the proceedings. He stopped combing his hair and drew himself up to his full height – four foot eleven. 'Yeah! Beat it kid.' Fishing in his pocket he drew out a sixpence. 'Here, take this. Treat yerself to the flicks.'

'Thank you.' Elfie took the sixpence politely. It was very kind of him. She knew he was not rich, and she did not want to offend him, and besides she could see anyway that she was not exactly welcome. Turning away, she made for the park gates and looked round. There was no sign of Jimmy and Margaret now. They must be lying down again. Jimmy would be Margaret's lover. It might even be more fun to have one like him that you could brag about to your friends, instead of Shonna's sort, the mystery lover that she would not give a name to. Jimmy was a bit small. Stunted, her mother called him. But he was real and he might even grow, in time.

Back home again Elfie amused herself by finding last year's school photo and cutting out pictures of herself and Shonna to put in the locket. It was difficult to get the size quite right, but after a lot of snipping, the job was done. It was a pity that her own head had half of Peggy's with it and Shonna's half of Sister Ignatious's. Shonna would not be too pleased about that. It was necessary, though, for the fit. It pleased her to think of herself and Shonna, face to face in the little locket. She closed it carefully and put it back in the box. Better to hide it away safely and not risk getting it lost again. They would stay in the locket, herself and Shonna, looking at each other for ever and ever. She nearly added

'Amen', but stopped herself in time. Shonna would not like that either.

Our Lady's feastday fell that year on a bank holiday. It was a beautiful day. Elfie's mother had declared there to be enough blue in the sky to make a cow a pair of trousers. The sun shone down on the Convent garden as the nuns and pupils got ready to celebrate.

All morning lorries had been arriving from Spalding with their cargo of flower petals. Masses and masses of them, to be strewn on the lawn in beautiful patterns, a different colour scheme each year. The design had been marked out on the grass in white paint, the gardeners working on it for two whole days. Now it was ready and they were spreading the petals with huge rakes into a carpet for the celebrants to walk across.

Elfie, as leader of the junior choir, was wearing her white organdie dress. It was now shorter and tighter than ever, but she did not care, she was too happy. She hopped up and down in excited anticipation. It was an honour to be taking part in this holy event. Shonna as a non-Catholic was only an observer and had to stand on the sidelines with Margaret.

No breeze even fluttered the petals. Every year it was the same. Our Lady seemed to have remarkable control over the weather. Elfie wondered what would happen if the wind got up. Would the petals take off like confetti and float up into the sky? And would the nuns give chase, their habits streaming behind them like bats? It would never happen of course. Our Lady would see to that. Elfie called across to Shonna and Margaret, 'Isn't it lovely?'

'It is and it ain't,' came Margaret's gloomy reply. 'It could be blooming unlucky, that's what.

'Why?' Elfie asked.

'Red and white are graveyard colours. Put them together and there'll be a death.'

'Rubbish,' said Shonna.

'It ain't rubbish. You ask me Aunty Shirley. Didn't she take red and white flowers to the hospital? Visited me grandpa. He said "Get that bleedin' lot out of here". That were with his last breath. Then he started to bleed. He bled and bled. There were gallons of it, running over the floor . . . out the door . . . down the corridor . . .'

'We only have nine pints,' Shonna pointed out.

'Well he were quite dried up,' Margaret continued undeterred. 'Like a husk. His coffin were so light it nearly blew away. No. You wouldn't catch me walking on them flowers. I'd be frit to death.'

Shonna stepped out and deliberately stood on the newly-strewn petals. She stared defiantly at Margaret. 'Your grandfather died because he was old. They do you know. It had nothing to do with red and white.'

'Says you.' Margaret was not convinced.

Shonna jumped up and down on the flowers. 'Cowardy cowardy custard!' She egged Margaret on to join her, but Margaret solemnly shook her head.

Sister Francis Assisi struck up a chord on the organ which had been dragged out on to the lawn, and Elfie ran to take her place at the head of the choir.

'Bring flowers of the fairest, bring blossoms the rarest, from garden and woodland and hillside and vale,' she sang, looking over her shoulder. Shonna was playing hopscotch on the petals now. Oh, why didn't one of the nuns see her? They all seemed to have their eyes downcast on their hymn books. Better keep to the grass verge as much as possible, and hope no one would notice. 'Queen of the Angels . . . and . . . Queen . . . of . . . the . . . May.'

The celebration over, Shonna cornered her in the cloak-room. 'Hey, listen you, I'm ready now. The big spell. You remember? The one I've been studying the book for. The one that's going to do away with *her* for good.'

Elfie thought about the petals. Shonna did not have any respect for anyone, not even Our Lady. She did not care who she got into trouble. 'I don't think I want to do it after all,' said Elfie.

'Yes you do. Of course you do. It'll be the most exciting thing you've ever done.' Shonna's tone became more wheedling. 'And I need you. Really I do. You're the only one that can help me. I'm not friends with any other Catholics. You can't let me down. We're blood brothers. Remember?'

'Well, what do you want me to do?'

'Get me some holy water. The real stuff, and two mass candles. Only you mustn't buy them. They have to be stolen or they lose their power.'

'But that's wicked.'

'Not really. Well, perhaps a little bit, but God will forgive you because you're so small. Just go to confession and He won't hold it against you. He'll definitely pardon you. If you don't believe that, you're not a good Catholic, are you?'

'But what are you going to do with them?'

'A really good spell. The most powerful one of all. Keep it to yourself. We'll tell Margaret at the end. When we're ready.'

'All right.' Elfie still felt a bit doubtful. 'But if I help you, will you play with me again?'

'Yes, yes. Of course. I haven't had time to play lately. I've been studying the book.'

'Please Shonna . . . tell me about it.'

Shonna looked around her carefully, then walked across the cloakroom to the row of toilets that lined the far wall and kicked open all the doors, revealing the miniature lavatory pans. The cubicles were empty. 'Can't be too careful. Those nuns are lurking everywhere. Now, swear on your mother's life that she'll die a horrible death if you tell anyone what I'm going to do.'

Elfie put her hand on her heart. 'I swear.'

Shonna lowered her voice. 'You write the name of the

person you want to harm on a piece of parchment in human blood. Then you sprinkle it with the Holy Water, after you've spat in it of course. You get the blood from your wrist. Then, and this is the tricky bit, you make a human sacrifice on an altar, just like Abraham did in the Bible. Then you bury the sacrifice and the parchment, and the person whose name is on it will meet with a terrible death. It's guaranteed.'

'We did a spell a bit like that before.'

'That was just a game. Kid's stuff. This is for real.'

'Who's going to be the sacrifice?'

'You!' Shonna pounced on her, and 'You You You' echoed round the tiles in the empty cloakroom.

'I'm not going to be a sacrifice.' Elfie cringed against the wall. 'You promised me I could help.'

'Only joking. Don't blub. You wouldn't be suitable anyway. It's got to be someone young and innocent. Perhaps a little kid. Or even a new-born baby.'

'Don't say that, Shonna. You know it makes me cry.'

'It says it in the book, I'm telling you. Look.' Shonna opened her satchel and took out the heavy velvet book, opening it at a place marked with a bus ticket, and pointed out a paragraph she had underlined.

CONCERNING THE VICTIM OF THE ART

Take your kid. Place it on a block with the throat turned upwards, so that it may be easier for you to cut it; be ready with your knife, and cut the throat at a single stroke, pronouncing the name of the spirit you wish to invoke. Have a care that two blows be not needed, but let it die at the first.

A black shape, keys jangling, appeared in the doorway. Sister Ignatious was about to lock up for the night. Shonna hastily stuffed the book back into her bag.

'And what are you two girls doing here after everyone else

has gone home?' Her eyes took in the bulging satchel. 'Now that's a nice fat bag you've got there Miss Creavy. Is it your books you're carrying, or something that you don't want me to know about?'

'It's just my homework Sister. I'm studying the crafts of the Middle Ages. I'm doing a test on them in June.'

'Is that so now?' Sister looked disbelieving. 'I thought 4B were doing the Wars of the Roses this term? Well get on your way now or your mothers will be worrying.' She swept away, her long black skirt swishing on the ground.

'It sounds a bit cruel,' said Elfie on the way home.

'Cruel? What do you mean? Pigs get their throats cut every day so you can have pork on a Sunday. You don't mind that, do you?' Shonna drew her finger across her throat and made a strangled noise. 'One blow and it's all over.'

Elfie grinned at her happily. It was a good game. They did have fun. No one else was as exciting as Shonna. Whatever would she do without her? She put her arm round Shonna's waist, happy just to be friends again.

Shonna didn't mention the spell again, or the sacrifice. It was as though the episode had never happened. She kept her promise to play with Elfie, and called every day after school. They walked in the park together and looked in the bushes for lovers that Shonna said were lurking there. They never found any, but they did see a man who smiled and beckoned. They kept looking from a distance and he called out, 'Come here girls and see what I've got.'

Shonna had laughed at him and shouted, 'We've seen them before. Go away or we'll tell the police.' Then she stood there staring at him until he dropped his eyes and turned and ran. Elfie had asked her what it was he was going to show them.

'Oh, just his thing,' Shonna replied. 'Little twerp! Didn't he run when I said about the police. We ought to look for some more and frighten them up.' She went further into the bushes, beating about with a stick, but there were no more men.

Shonna was being very kind to Elfie. Once she even took her to the children's matinée at the picture house and paid sixpence for her to go in. And when Elfie was bullied at school for being fat, Shonna had jumped to her defence like a true friend. As the month passed and no more was said about the spell, Elfie stopped worrying. It was silly to get upset about something that could never happen. Nobody would trust Shonna with a baby even if they did not know what she planned to do with it. She had often knocked on doors and asked mothers if she could take their babies for a walk, but the answer was always 'No'. Now Margaret could often be seen in the park or the High Street with a pram and a contented infant on board. Mothers trusted Margaret, thinking her a capable girl. Margaret, however, would not lend a baby to Shonna. She guarded them with her life. And there was the one that Nora Adora was supposed to be having, but they had not heard much about it lately. Every time Elfie and Margaret asked when it was going to be ready Shonna replied, 'Not yet.' Margaret said Nora must be going round for a second time.

Suddenly, Shonna started acting strangely all over again. She kept disappearing for days on end, and when seen across the street or in the assembly hall, she would make rocking movements with her arms as though cradling a baby. Once, when no one was looking except Elfie, she drew a finger across her throat from ear to ear, and grinned. And at the 'Children of Mary' gathering Elfie saw her playing with the little knife, snapping the blade open and shut in full view of Sister Ignatious, who had said, 'If you wish to sharpen your pencil Shonna, please use the proper tool, and put that knife back wherever you got it from. Don't let me see it again.' Elfie had plucked up the courage, at playtime, to ask for the knife.

'What knife?' said Shonna, and staggered about the playground saying, 'Is this a dagger that I see before me?' She had the cheek to pretend she did not know what Elfie was talking about.

Now Elfie began to have doubts. Perhaps Shonna meant what she said after all, and was laying plans for the spell. Perhaps she ought to tell on her. It might sound silly to a grown-up though, as if she had made the whole thing up. They would never believe a little girl of nine, and Shonna was very convincing. If only Elfie had some proof. The only thing she could do would be to make some plans herself to try to prevent it from happening. She would pretend to go along with the idea and then, at the last minute, snatch the baby and run home with it. She could probably hide it in the attic, since no one went there any more. At least not since the day Shonna had trodden on the plaster between the rafters and a piece of the ceiling had come down. Anyway, even if her mother found the baby, she would be sure to love it, and help Elfie look after it. The baby would take the place of June and they need not go to the cemetery any more.

Elfie started hoarding things, occupying her spare time knitting a scarf in brightly coloured wool stripes. An old blanket that had belonged to her as a baby was retrieved from the rag bag, and stored with a tin of condensed milk and a cushion under her bed. If she could only get her hands on the *Chronicle*, there were some patterns for baby clothes in it. But Shonna had the book. Of course if she went on a Saturday afternoon when all the Creavys were out, it would be easy. A copy could be made on tracing paper and no one would ever know. She knew that Shonna played tennis now with her father on Saturdays, and Mrs Creavy went to the 'Home and Colonial'.

After lunch on Saturday Elfie hid in the privet hedge that surrounded the Creavys' garden and watched until she saw them come out. Shonna wore a smart pleated tennis skirt, while Mr

Creavy's pinstripes ended in white plimsolls. They carried tennis rackets and a string net of balls, and he had his arm round Shonna's shoulders. Elfie felt a pang of envy. Her own father played bowls with a lot of old men on Saturday afternoon, and did not care if she felt lonely. Then Mrs Creavy came out, a basket on each arm. She scurried along looking at the pavement, reminding Elfie in a funny sort of way of the peahen in the park, drab and grey, scurrying round her colourful mate. Perhaps she had changed a lot since the day she had run off with Mr Creavy. Second sight might be a very sad thing to have. Elfie thought of her mother's saying, 'What you don't know, you don't worry about'. Mrs Creavy always seemed very worried; perhaps she knew a lot more than she wanted to.

Knowing she was being naughty, her heart beating fast, Elfie looked round to see if anyone was watching, and then trotted up the gravel drive and in through the side door. No one in Arcadia Road locked their doors. If anyone caught her, she would say she was waiting for Shonna to come back.

The kitchen looked as bright and cheery as ever. No sign now of the wreckage they had caused last year. Elfie thought about Mrs Creavy's fondness for polishing. That mess must have made her very happy. She lifted the heavy book off the dresser and set it on the floor, humming 'Some Day My Prince Will Come' and thinking about Nora and Mr Creavy. She imagined Nora opening the door of the mill in the swansdown wrap. When she grew up she would have one just like it and wear it all the time, except to church. But perhaps Mr Creavy did not see Nora anymore. He was spending more time with Shonna lately, and that might be a good thing because then Shonna would drop that dreadful plan, and Nora could marry the American Army Officer, and she, Elfie, would be their bridesmaid and everyone would be happy ever after. Well, she would just copy the patterns anyway. Better to be prepared. Elfie flicked over the pages. 'DANCING AS A SOCIAL AID' caught her attention. She read on:

Today the man or woman who cannot dance is regarded as a social outcast. There are few restaurants and hotels that do not make a feature of dancing; every parish has its quota of dance halls, whilst it would be difficult to find even the smallest village in which dancing does not take place. Therefore those who do not dance, particularly among the fair sex, must be looked upon as outcasts.

She could not dance. Not a step. Her mother said she had two left feet. Shonna went to ballet lessons at Miss Garner's. She used to wear her little satin slippers slung round her neck on the way home to show where she had been. Even Margaret, with no lessons at all, could do a fair old tango with the yard brush. Was that why they were all out having fun, while she was alone on a Saturday afternoon, copying patterns of pilch knickers on tracing paper? It didn't matter how clever you were, if you were top of the class and could recite 'The Little Peach' all the way through, if you had not got dancing you were an outcast. Now where was that bit on 'Home Management'?

A muffled noise from within the house startled her. It sounded like a door closing. The stairs creaked. Elfie ran across the kitchen and opened the kitchen door a fraction to listen. Silence. It must have been her imagination. She returned to the book and knelt down, starting to draw. She traced the picture of a baby's vest and pilch, under which was written:

The daintiest garments imaginable may be cut for baby from the best part of celanese knickers, when they are outgrown or outworn. When fresh from the laundry, cut them open at the seams and . . .

There was the noise again. This time she was certain. It was a sort of creaking as though someone was walking overhead. But everyone was out; she had watched them go. Who could it be? A ghost! A burglar! Perhaps she ought to run away, but Elfie felt she had to know. If she just crept quietly up the stairs and peeped it would do no harm. Wouldn't Shonna be pleased with her if she caught a burglar. Well, not caught him, she couldn't do that. Just take a peek at him, and tell Shonna what he looked like. She might even be able to draw him on the tracing paper and then boast about what *she* did on a Saturday afternoon.

Very quietly Elfie opened the kitchen door and slipped out. She crept to the foot of the stairs. Yes, there were definitely sounds coming from above. Low voices. Were there two of them? She felt a bit less confident. Perhaps it was better not to try and draw them, just see who it was and run away quickly, and tell a policeman.

Crawling up the stairs on the thick carpet, Elfie lay flat, her chin resting on the top step. All the heavy oak doors were shut tight and a trail of clothes was scattered untidily along the passage to the front bedroom: a white skirt; another garment, pink, crumpled in a ball; one plimsoll. There were rufflings and creakings behind the door, and muffled voices, a giggle. Had Mrs Creavy returned early from the 'Home and Colonial'? No, she would surely have come straight into the kitchen, and was not giggly by any stretch of the imagination. It couldn't be her. Elfie knew she should run away, but her feet seemed glued to the ground. Grown-ups did such funny things in bedrooms. Shonna had said so. Jumping naked on someone could make you giggle . . . if you didn't die of shame first. Certainly someone had come in. That first noise she had heard. Was it Shonna and Mr Creavy? Those looked rather like Shonna's clothes; but they wouldn't be in the bedroom together, would they? Since Elfie had found out about grown-ups' strange behaviour she had seen them in a new light. She only had to look at people now to see them without their clothes and jumping on each other. Her mind seemed to be filled with them. Once or twice she had had strange fits of laughing. Even looking at her parents had triggered one off and she had been sent from the table. Sometimes just thinking about such things gave her a funny feeling in the pit of her stomach. About to sneeze, Elfie realized her face was pressed to the floor and fluff was going up her nose, and she had dribbled a mark on the carpet. Better get off home quickly before she was discovered. She slid the whole length of the stairs, her stomach going bumpity bump on each step. When she reached the bottom she got up and ran to the front door, struggling with the latch, then dashed to the kitchen for her tracing book before racing up the road. As she ran she remembered with trepidation Shonna's words. *Before I try it for myself.*

Elfie turned towards the park. If she's there, then everything is all right, she thought. I'm just a bad girl even thinking such things. That's a sin. At the Convent it was drummed into them every day, they must not have impure thoughts. Up till now she had not known what they were. Oh please, oh please God, make Shonna be playing tennis.

The ground was so hot she could feel it through her thin sandals, and a heat haze seemed to be rising from the grass. A few couples were spread out on their backs, taking advantage of this spell of the good weather, and a group of children sat lethargically on a bench, too hot to play. Surely there would be a storm tonight. Out of breath with running, Elfie slowed down as she neared the tennis courts and saw with disappointment that they were all empty. Only two young men sat on the grass nearby, dark patches of sweat showing at the armpits of their sports shirts, their rackets slung aside. No sign of Shonna and Mr Creavy. Feeling heavy with worry, she set off again for home. As she neared the park gates she saw them in front of her in a shimmer of heat. Elfie's hair clung moistly to her head and she pushed it out of her eyes.

'Shonna! Shonna!' she shouted and raced for the entrance. 'Wait for me. Wait for me.' Head down she bumped straight into a man coming the other way. He grabbed her by the shoulder, and shook her lightly.

'Look where you're going, girl.'

Elfie struggled to free herself from his grasp. It was the old man from the bus queue. 'Let me go. Please let me go,' she shouted.

'What's happened to manners these days,' he said sharply. 'What's the word?'

'Sorry, I'm sorry. I'm running to catch my friend. I can see her up the road.'

'Then you've better eyesight than I have,' the man answered, releasing her. Elfie looked, but apart from a lady walking her dog, the long road home was empty.

She ran to her room and dived under the bed, put her arms up over her ears and shut her eyes tightly to make the stars and patterns come, but still waxy pink figures jumped about in her brain doing the most distressing things, and they all looked like Shonna and Mr Creavy. She stayed hunched there a long time, getting stiff and cold.

Her mother shouted that tea was ready, and when Elfie did not come, Mrs Brown looked for her and found her still under the bed. She told her not to be silly, and to come out.

'If that girl's been upsetting you again I'll go and see her mother. Blessed if I'd play with someone who kept making me cry. Can't you find a more suitable friend?' Then Mrs Brown went on and on about asking Father Dominic if there were any nice girls in the orphanage who could be brought around to play. 'It's come to something, if we've got to go to the poorhouse to find you a friend.'

Elfie did not move and at last had to be dragged out by her father. She refusd to speak or tell them what was wrong. She could not say anything. If she even mentioned a naked person, they would surely have her put away. Elfie kept her eyes tight shut. Mr Brown said perhaps the doctor ought to be sent for. Was it about her monthly time?

'Nonsense. She's far too young. Just remember that doctors cost money and we're not on the panel. Remember the last time?' Mrs Brown reminded her husband that the child was highly-strung, and had always been hysterical. Bed and a frightening powder were all that was called for; everything would look different in the morning.

11

The queue was only moving forward at a snail's pace, so who had been extra wicked this week? It would be nice, thought Elfie, if someone had a really whopping deadly sin to confess, because it would make her own less noticeable. She looked along the row of girls in their neat gymslips and white cotton blouses, hair cut short or pigtailed like her own. They did not look as if they had a good sin between them. A boring lot of girls. At the worst, cribbing an exam, and probably only snitching a pencil rubber. Boys might have been better, but then of course they went to confession at a different time, so that even their sins did not mingle with those of the girls.

Elfie had manoeuvred herself into last position, a difficult task because it was a well-known fact that the penances got shorter as the priest's suppertime got closer, and the fight for last place could be dirty, with lots of shoving and pinching and treading on toes. And for the last one in the queue there was less chance of anyone earwigging at the door.

Elfie knew she had to confess. She had so many sins now that she did not know quite where to begin, and hoped she would not get them muddled. She started to list them in her mind. Stealing: that was the Holy Water. She was glad she had left the candles alone – Shonna could get those herself.

Being an accessory: that was in the Catechism. It was all to do with knowing about someone doing something naughty and not trying to stop them. Of course, she need not mention the sacrifice, because that was not a sin. The Bible was full of them. Abraham was going to sacrifice Isaac, or was it the other way about? Elfie was getting very muddled. Last week she would have known quite clearly which was which, but so much had happened since then. Then there was Moses. Was he a sacrifice? She was not too sure. Anyway he might have been if someone had not fished him out of the bulrushes. The evening sunlight streamed through the stained-glass window, sending little points of light shooting from the hands out-stretched on the cross. *He* was a sacrifice too, wasn't he?

Now there was this other sin, the difficult one, the one about impure thoughts. That was going to be tricky to talk about. Shonna had said, though, that the priest would forgive her anything because she was only a little girl. She hoped she sounded little, because of course he would not be able to see her. That had once seemed like a good thing, but right now she wanted to be seen being little. Suffer little children.

Looking down at the highly-polished floor Elfie saw the pale moon of her face reflected there. Then behind it rose another face. Shonna's! She looked round, expecting to see the girl standing behind her, but there was no one there because she was the last in the queue. The other face had faded, like the Cheshire cat. Just sunlight playing tricks.

The child in front of Elfie came out of the box, head bowed, looking smug. The sort of girl my mother would ask round to play, she thought. Perhaps she had better not say too much about Shonna, in case the priest let it slip to her mother. Mummy did talk to them a lot. You never knew what they were saying. What a pity one had to confess at all. No good trying to dodge it though. It was there and you had to do it. The alternative was going to hell. Hitler was surely going there, and Goebbels and Hess and the whole bang lot of them.

Daddy had said so. Of course you could get purgatory for lesser sins. There were no flames there. You just suffered a sense of loss, and Elfie knew what that was like from when baby June died, and when Mummy or Shonna would not speak to her. Sister Francis gave her a shove in the back. 'Wake up child. You're dreaming. The Father's waiting.'

Elfie entered the confessional and knelt down on the little hassock on the shelf below the grill. When the priest slid the shutter back it reminded her of the budgie's cage, with him inside there perhaps with his head cocked on one side, listening. It was funny talking to someone you could not see. Was this how blind people felt? And was he thinking the same sort of thoughts as her, about cages and budgies and things other than sins. She put her hand over her mouth before a giggle escaped. It seemed too much to hope that he would be a stranger, but that would be safer.

'Bless me Father for I have sinned . . .' she began.

The priest cut her short. 'And what have you been doing to upset Jesus this week?' he asked briskly. It was Father Dominic. Nobody could mistake his Irish brogue.

'I took some Holy Water, Father.' There! It was out. It was easier than she had thought. She would just wait now for the number of 'Hail Marys' she would have to say.

But the priest said, 'And why did you take it?'

'I just wanted some. I took it home with me in a paste jar.' That did not sound so good. It made it sound cheap. Elfie was sure, too, that somewhere she had heard that Holy Water represented the fluid that flowed from Jesus's side when the spear was thrust in.

The priest went on, 'Well that's not a bad thing to be wanting the Holy Water, but it belongs to the church. We must be careful not to take what doesn't belong to us. Neither is it right or respectful that such a Blessed Thing be carried around in a . . . paste jar. If you want some, you must bring a suitable container – you can buy them at the Catholic shop next to the cathedral – along with a little sponge to hang on your wall. Ask your mother to get you one. I believe they do sell various brands of water too. A lot of people favour that from Lourdes. Now what else is worrying you?'

'I have impure thoughts Father. About my friend.'

There was a very long pause. Elfie wondered if he had gone away. There was another door at the back, wasn't there? But at last he spoke. 'How old are you child?'

'I've just turned nine Father.'

'And who is your friend? Is he a Catholic boy?'

'No Father. He isn't a boy. He's a girl.'

There was a much longer pause this time. He really must have gone away. Had she said something terribly wrong? Would it have been better to say it was Peter Collins from a good Catholic family? But she had never had any impure thoughts about him. Whenever he came into her mind he was always fully-dressed and carrying his satchel. The priest's voice broke in on her thoughts.

'Is this, er, girl, older than you child?' Now what difference did that make? Sins did not get bigger as you got older. Once you were past the age of reason a sin was a sin, everyone knew that.

'Yes Father,' Elfie answered. 'She's thirteen.' Shonna had celebrated her birthday last week having dinner at a big hotel with her father. Elfie had been disappointed that there had been no party, but Shonna had told her she was too old for that sort of thing now.

'It's a difficult age, child. You mustn't let her lead you into anything unchaste. Try not to be alone with her, and pray for strength to resist temptation. Encourage her in healthy out-door pursuits, like swimming, or tennis. Say three "Hail Marys" and an "Our Father" and the Blessed Virgin will help you. I will pray for you too.' He started to pronounce the 'Nunc Dimitti', and she gave a sigh of relief as she half-listened to the words. What had he said? 'Don't be alone with her.'

Well, that wasn't too difficult. She usually saw Shonna at school, or else Margaret was with them. He hadn't said she must not see Shonna at all, even in her thoughts.

Elfie bowed her head dutifully as Father Dominic blessed her, mumbled 'Thank you Father' and came out of the box, blinking in the bright evening sunlight. It was over, and when Shonna called her for the spell, her conscience would be clear. Sister Francis grabbed her by the arm, her sharp thin fingers digging into Elfie's soft flesh.

'What a long time you were in there. You must have had a lot to confess. We thought you were a good little girl. It just goes to show, doesn't it? And the Father with his lamb chops burning and his potatoes frizzled.'

12

Elfie lay in bed, straight like a corpse, her hands by her sides. She had this feeling that if she lay quite still and hardly breathed her parents would settle down and go to sleep quicker. It did not seem to be working though, and she could still hear creakings and whispers. Soon Margaret would be waiting outside in the shadow of the hedge. It was so easy for Margaret to get out on a Friday night because her mother and Aunty Shirley would be up the American camp, dancing with the soldiers. They never missed a week. Margaret could do what she liked. She boasted that Jim had stayed with her till three o'clock in the morning last week. As Jim never had very much to say, there must have been a lot of French kissing. Elfie kept looking into Margaret's eyes to see if she could see changes, like Shonna had told her she would, but Margaret's eyes still looked their normal close-together selves, only a bit shifty lately. Now there was silence. Elfie held her breath, letting it out in little short spurts, as she listened. A gentle snoring sound started.

She crept out of bed, still fully-dressed in her school uniform, and went quietly down the stairs. In her hand was a little paper bag of clothes that she had taken off the china doll and the precious paste jar. There was no way of knowing if the baby would be dressed. It might catch cold if she brought it home in the night air naked. Chilly air could damage your kidneys; you should wear something warm next to your skin. Shonna might ask what was in the bag, and if Elfie refused to tell her, it could cause a fight. The preparations might keep Shonna occupied though, and too busy to notice.

Margaret was crouched under the hedge. She was so thin you could hardly see her. She was one of those girls that Elfie's mother said had to stand twice to cast a shadow. Perhaps she did not get enough to eat; they did not have much money. Elfie whispered, 'Where's Molly?'

Margaret clapped her hand over Elfie's mouth. Not roughly, but to warn her not to talk. They crept along the fences, keeping low. It was very exciting, and so dark. One or two chinks in the blackout curtains told them that life was still going on behind them, otherwise you wouldn't have known. When they were a good distance up the road, Margaret said, 'Molly's asleep. I couldn't wake her, but Tom will be in soon.'

Fancy leaving Molly in the house alone. Say she woke up and played with matches. Elfie shuddered, but said nothing. You couldn't tell Margaret anything, she was a bit of a know-all. Well, it was her sister. They reached Shonna's gate and Elfie was about to turn in, when Margaret dragged her past it. Mr Creavy's bicycle was standing in the drive. It looked lost and lonely without him. It was the sort of drive that should have a big glossy car in it, not a bicycle. Then Margaret led her, not up Shonna's drive, but up the one next door, until they got level with the outside lavatory, which stood a short way from the house. The neighbours must be having a party, thought Elfie. She could hear gramophone music and sounds of laughter. Other people led such happy lives. She could not imagine her parents, or any of her relatives, ever dancing to the gramophone, even if they had one. Elfie crept up to the window to listen, and started to hum 'South Of the Border' along with the music. Margaret hushed her quickly, and then squeezed through a small gap in the fence. Elfie followed, but got stuck. Her bottom was just too big. 'Trust you,' whispered Margaret as she prised the two pieces of fencing apart. 'Blast it. I've got creosote on me hands and it smells horrible.'

Elfie pushed her way through. 'I think I've got a splinter.'

'Where?'

'In my bottom.'

'Well that's all right,' said Margaret. 'You won't be sitting on it again tonight, will you? And your mother can get it out with a hot needle in the morning.'

The lavatory door opened a crack and Shonna peeped out. 'Where have you been?' she whispered crossly. 'I thought you were never coming.' She pulled the door open wider and let them in.

'Give us a chance,' said Margaret. 'It ain't that easy for Elf to get out you know. Her old folk watch her like hawks.' They crowded themselves into the confines of the small room.

'Next door is having a party,' Margaret said.

'Good. They'll be busy with their own affairs and not nosing into ours,' said Shonna, who was in her nightdress and had bare feet. She told them she had come out of the bedroom window on a rope. They did not believe her. She could just walk down the stairs, couldn't she?

'What's in the bag Elfie?' Shonna asked.

'Nothing.' Elfie looked guilty and Shonna shot her a suspicious look and put her hand out. Margaret slapped it down. 'Get on with it,' she said, 'or me Mum'll be back.'

'All right, all right. Keep your shirt on. Everything's ready.'

Shonna reached up and drew the blackout curtain across the slit window, and Elfie was surprised to see that she no longer had to stand on the lavatory seat to do so. As she reached up her developing breasts were outlined against the thin silk of her nightie, which now ended half-way down her calves. She isn't a child any more, Elfie thought. She's a young woman now and very beautiful. I wish I looked like that. She's just like a ballet dancer, and her eyelashes are so long I can see their shadows on her cheeks. I shall put Vaseline on my eyes every night to make my lashes grow. Elfie gave a long envious sigh and Shonna turned on her.

'What are you huffing and puffing about? You sound out of breath. Why don't you go on a diet?'

'She can't help being fat,' Margaret chipped in. 'It is heredity you know. It's all in yer glands, see. Some have them, some don't. Me Aunty Shirley's got 'em and they bother her no end. So don't go making her cry and getting her upset or we'll be here half the blooming night.'

Elfie squeezed her hand gratefully. Margaret was very comforting. Then she looked round the lavatory. It somehow seemed smaller and more cramped than last year, or was that because they had all grown? Her head was level with Margaret's armpits. Elfie turned her nose away fastidiously; Margaret should wear dress shields.

Apart from themselves, and Mr Creavy's oilskins hanging up behind the door, the lavatory was almost empty. No sign of a baby, unless it was in the laundry basket standing beside the seat. That had not been there before. It had a lid on it, so if there was a baby in there, it might not be able to breathe. Elfie would not put it past Shonna not to care about that. Perhaps there was no baby. That would surely spoil the spell and then Nora Adora, whom she admired so much, would be safe. It would just become another of Shonna's games. Elfie wondered why she felt disappointed. It was the wrong feeling to have. Perhaps she had hoped too much for the baby. It all seemed a bit silly now. Of course there wouldn't be one, and if there was she wouldn't be allowed to keep it. Someone would be crying for it, most likely its mother. Anyway it was doubtful if Shonna would have let her run away with it; on account of her being so quick and so strong, she would never let her get out of the door. Elfie put the paste pot on the shelf and held the bag of doll's clothes behind her back, trying to think herself into being thin and invisible, so that Shonna would not notice her so much. But Shonna was not bothering with her. She jumped down off the seat, and stretched one arm out in front of her in a Nazi salute.

'Right! Let's kill the bitch! People like her shouldn't be allowed to live.'

'Heil Hitler!' Margaret responded. 'Weren't he on the Pathe news last week? We've all got a right to live you know.'

Shonna took no notice and went on, 'First we sprinkle the place with Holy Water.' She turned to Elfie, 'I hope you brought it.'

Elfie pointed to the paste pot on the ledge. Margaret nudged her. 'Did you wash it first Elf? Shrimp paste goes off mighty quick in the hot weather. It could be really smelly by now.' Margaret should talk.

'All the better,' said Shonna. 'It says in the book that the skin should be fumigated with stinking odours. The more it pongs, the better. Give me the parchment.'

Margaret handed her an ancient scroll. 'You'll have to write on the back, cos there's a lot of old rubbish scrawled on the front in a funny language.'

Shonna turned the parchment over carefully, it was quite brittle. 'Where did you get this?'

'In the museum. I hid in the mummy's case till the keeper had gone by.'

It had made headlines in the local paper. 'Ancient Egyptian Papyrus Stolen From Town Museum.' But apart from Pop-Eye and their stars, Shonna and Margaret did not read the papers. Now Shonna patted Margaret's hand. 'Good girl. I shall write her name round it in a circle . . .' She paused for effect, then went on in very sombre tones, '. . . in human blood. Then I shall perform the sacrifice.'

'What sacrifice?' said Margaret. 'You can't make no sacrifice in here. You have to have an altar or a bonfire or a summit.'

'I have one,' said Shonna, looking sly. Elfie started to tremble. It all came back to her, the things that she had tried to put from her mind. How really daring Shonna was. She was bold enough to do anything.

'Yes,' Shonna went on. 'I've got a real sacrifice. Already prepared. A human one.' Margaret started to giggle.

'A new-born baby,' Shonna rapped out.

Margaret stopped giggling and stared at Shonna, mouth open. She looks a bit like Molly now, thought Elfie, it must run in the family, like Mummy said. Margaret pulled herself together. 'What baby?' she asked.

'There's one in here,' said Shonna. 'In this basket.'

'Says you.' It was Margaret's turn to look superior now. 'Show us it. Or we'll all go home.'

Shonna moved to where the basket stood and threw the lid open with a flourish. Then she picked up a small flannel-wrapped bundle and held it aloft. Margaret stretched up and tried to grab it, but Shonna was too tall for her and held it teasingly out of reach, fending her off with her free hand.

Margaret doubled up with laughter. 'You slay me!' she said. 'I'll wet me blinking self laughing in a minute if you don't give over. It's a doll! That's what it is! You great big booby! You're playing with dolls!'

Shonna spoke through clenched teeth. 'Keep your voice down will you. Do you want all the neighbours to hear? Anyway, you can say what you like, but *she* knows the truth.' She stabbed the air in the direction of the terrified Elfie.

What a pair they are, Margaret thought. Elfie, just a dumb little kid standing there shivering with fright, and Shonna almost ready for the loony bin. She had stood Jim up tonight for this. Two kids who were planning to sacrifice a doll. It was all right for Elfie – she was still a small girl – but it was time Shonna knew better. She should get herself a real fellow, instead of mooning over an imaginary lover. Get stuck into the facts of life and give her mind a rest from this silly nonsense. Margaret yawned and leaned against the lavatory wall, prepared to be bored. She took a crumpled cigarette butt out of her pocket and lit it. 'Just get on with it then.'

Shonna placed the little bundle on the back of the lavatory seat and put the lid up to hide it. Then she lit the two candles which she had painted black. They smoked and spluttered, and the paint gave off an acrid smell. Shonna unscrewed the top of the paste pot and spat into it, and then sprinkled the water about liberally, making the candles splutter even more. Elfie's eyes started to smart, she wished Shonna was not so fond of candlelight, as it was very uncomfortable. Shonna surveyed the scene, looking satisfied, and then turned to face them. 'Take your clothes off,' she ordered.

'Why?'

'Because the art of infernal necromancy requires you to be naked.' Shonna snatched at Elfie's blouse. 'I said take your clothes off, all of them.'

Elfie dropped the bag of doll's clothes and clutched at her collar with both hands, back pressed against the wall.

'No,' she squealed. 'I can't. It's rude.'

'Well I can't take mine off,' said Margaret. 'Wrong time of the month. I've got me visitors. It wouldn't be decent.'

'Well don't then. Spoil it all. See if I care!'

Shonna stripped off her nightdress and flung it to the floor. Elfie stared at her, shocked. She did not look anything like the Shonna she had pictured, and dreamed about. That one was all smooth and pink like a doll, its legs ending in a neat 'V' shape at the top. The real Shonna stood there, white and slim, with a thick tuft of pubic hair where the 'V' should be. Elfie had never seen anyone undressed before, besides herself. She slid down the wall and crouched on her haunches, staring from under Margaret's arm, fascinated by the sight. Elfie then looked up at Margaret to see if she was surprised too. Margaret was yawning.

Shonna closed her eyes, but neither of them moved in case she was still peeping. She chanted:

'O Lord, who didst make all things in wisdom; who didst choose Abraham, Thy first believer, and his seed which hath multiplied like the stars in heaven; who didst appear to Moses, Thy servant, surrounded by flaming fires; I humbly beseech Thy mercy, Praying to Thee to consecrate this skin by Thy virtue, O most Holy Adonai, whose reign endureth forever, Amen.'

Holding the parchment up to her lips, Shonna made a great show of kissing it.

'Come on for gawd's sake. Do hurry it up. That's enough of the old mumbo-jumbo.' Shifting her weight to her other foot Margaret looked down at the cigarette butt between her fingers, now burned to a tiny stub, and wondered if she had time to light up another.

Elfie's eyes were fixed on the lavatory seat, behind which lay the precious bundle. Should she make a grab for it now, while Shonna's eyes were still closed? It must be very small to lie there so still. It was not what she had expected. In her dreams she had always seen a big bouncing baby, like the one advertising Pear's soap. Margaret must be right. It was a doll. Babies could not breathe through blankets, could they?

Shonna's eyes snapped open, reminding Elfie of bits of green glass. She delved into the basket again and came up with the tortoiseshell knife, and waved it at Margaret, who was chewing her nails.

'Give that to me. It's mine,' Elfie pleaded.

Shonna glared at her. 'No it isn't. It's out of my manicure set. You lost yours that day at the mill, spying on my father.'

Elfie watched, defeated, as Shonna dipped into the basket again. What now? This time she came up with a pigeon's feather, sharpened into a quill.

Margaret's eyes were just slits. 'Cut the dramatics. What were your dad doing at the mill?'

'Nothing.'

'Oh yes he were. I bet he were doing that red-haired bit. I bet he were.' Margaret laughed nastily. 'Your dad is a lech. Me Aunty Shirley says so. I've heard tell your dad is mustard.'

Shonna ignored her. 'I shall draw blood and write the vixen's name on the parchment. I shall write it in a circle till the letters meet.' Kneeling in front of the lavatory she placed her arm on the seat, palm upwards, and scratched her wrist with the blade. The grazed skin turned red. Shonna pressed the wound to make the blood run, but nothing happened.

'At least your dad has more go in him than you. I don't believe you have got a lover at all,' Margaret continued.

Shonna forced the knife a little deeper into her arm, but still there was only the merest trickle of blood.

Margaret looked on sceptically, while Elfie felt a peculiar sense of foreboding. 'Muff this spell and we'll never listen to you again . . .' Margaret began. Shonna shot her a look that could kill.

'Cowardy cowardy custard, face like a ha'porth of mustard!' Margaret jeered. 'You've hardly touched yourself!' Her pinched little face looked mean as she taunted Shonna, and she lit up another butt.

'OK, you'll see who's yellow,' Shonna snarled. She drew in a deep breath, bit into her lower lip and stabbed the knife hard into her wrist.

Arterial blood shot upwards in a little fountain, coming out in short spurts and tippling over, splashing softly on the quarry-tiled floor. They all watched it in silence, hypnotized, as it kept on spurting. Then Shonna clapped her other hand over her wrist. The blood slid through her fingers. When Shonna opened her mouth to scream Elfie was surprised that so little sound came out. It was like screaming in a dream, but it jolted Margaret into action. She pulled at Elfie's gymslip sash but it stuck in the loops and would not come off. Margaret struggled with it, almost cutting Elfie in half, and freed it with a jerk that sent her spinning into the wall. Grabbing hold of Shonna, Margaret tied the belt round the top of her arm and ran out.

Now she'll get help, thought Elfie. Everything will be all right. I hope they won't be too cross. But within seconds Margaret had returned alone, and started scrabbling on the floor. Shonna shrieked, 'What are you doing? Get help! Do you hear me? Get my dad!' Elfie watched as Margaret retrieved her cigarette butts and put them in her pocket. 'You'd better run off home,' she said to Elfie, and was gone again.

The night was warm and sticky, but Elfie shivered as she hovered in the doorway. It might be a good idea to do as Margaret said. She would be bringing grown-ups and they would be angry. Someone would be sure to tell her mother, and that would be the end of playing with Shonna for good. She did not want to leave her alone either, or miss finding out what was in the bundle. Shonna was naked too, and that was not right. Elfie crept forward and picked up the nightie, but as she draped it round the bare shoulders, Shonna slipped to the floor, her red curls mingling with the blood. She was crying, not loudly, but in a scared sort of way, in little squeaks. The gymslip sash had fallen off and was lying on the floor, a black ineffectual circle.

Elfie whispered, 'Hold on Shonna. Margaret won't be long.' A voice that did not even sound like Shonna anymore, but like a very little girl, answered, 'Don't go Elfie, please don't go.' Then the candle flickered and burnt out. In the darkness Elfie lost all sense of time. Why was it darkness made time seem longer? Where was Margaret? Was she having trouble finding someone? Of course, they might all be in bed. Wouldn't they be surprised? If they didn't hear Margaret knocking would she just give up and go home? Margaret could be very unreliable. Elfie began to wish that she had never come. Gingerly she put out her hand and touched Shonna. Why was her skin so cold and damp? 'Don't cry,' she whispered, even though the crying had stopped.

Then a harsh light flooded the small room as a back door opened in the neighbouring house. The gramophone music reached Elfie's ears. Bertha Willmott rolling out the barrel now in true British style. Shonna was still on the floor. Elfie had half expected her to have disappeared, and find it was all a bad dream. But Shonna was so quiet now. Perhaps she had fallen asleep. Elfie whispered urgently, 'Shonna! Shonna! Wake up . . . please.' A voice from outside shouted 'Put that light out' and everything went dark again.

Footsteps scrunching on the gravel were running from the direction of the house. Margaret had wakened someone at last. Elfie was glad now that she had stayed. Mr Creavy would surely be pleased with her for keeping Shonna company and covering her nakedness. But as the torch beam searched round the lavatory and lit them up, Mr Creavy pushed her roughly aside and fell on his knees beside Shonna. Then he gathered her up in his arms, and made for the house. 'You get off home,' he shouted over his shoulder.

Elfie did not move. She stood by the lavatory door feeling hurt and rejected, watching him stride up the garden path, Shonna's head dropping back over his arm as though her neck was broken. Mrs Creavy appeared in the light of the kitchen door. She did not seem to be worried about the blackout. Elfie could hear Margaret shouting that they had just been playing and it was only a bit of witchcraft, just a game. Margaret was wrong, wasn't she? It wasn't a game at all. Something terrible had happened. Elfie knew it had because Mrs Creavy had started to scream when she saw Shonna. Loud thin piercing screams, like Elfie's mother had made when June had died. Elfie put her hands over her ears to muffle the sounds and she shut her eyes tight. But now the stars and coloured lights would not come. Only pictures of Shonna flashed in her brain. Pretty laughing Shonna, making up games to amuse them. Shonna with her eyes closed, dreaming of her phantom lover. Shonna, her best friend, who was never ever going to die.

When Elfie opened her eyes, the kitchen door was shut. She did not know if Margaret was still there, or if she had been sent away. Perhaps she had better creep off home herself. There was still the bundle on the lavatory seat, though. She had better have a peep and see what was in it. Creeping into the lavatory, she felt behind the toilet lid and pulled the basket out. It landed with a soft thunk on the floor, and she toed it gently to the door to look at it in the light from the house, unwrapping it very carefully. It was not a doll. Of course it wasn't.

Three years ago Elfie's father had taken his daughter by the hand and led her into the parlour for a last look at June. Here was a similar little face with tightly-screwed up eyes, its tiny body wrapped in swaddling clothes, like a miniature mummy. All of a sudden Elfie knew where Shonna had got the baby from. Mr Creavy must work in that funeral place up the alley. Elfie remembered seeing Shonna's legs disappearing through the window, and the pale thin hand waving to her. It had been Mr Creavy's, of course! Shonna must have stolen the poor dead baby when he was not looking. Shonna would think it was a really good joke. Elfie could imagine her looking round to see their faces; she loved to shock them.

In Elfie's ears echoed Margaret's words about a good Christian burial for poor little souls that had never drawn a breath. Elfie shuddered and covered the small still face with the blanket, so as not to have to look any more. She made up her mind to get rid of it, before *they* found out. She could hardly go and knock on the door with it, saying 'Please Mr Creavy, Shonna's left this.' And to leave it behind would be to betray Shonna. She would never do that. Everything had gone wrong; if only it could have been like that night with the rose. The memory of it still excited her.

Then Elfie knew what she must do. Looking around for something to wrap the bundle in, she took Mr Creavy's yellow sou'wester from the peg, and popped the baby inside. It made Elfie feel all cringy to touch it. Keeping in the shadow of the bushes, she ran down the path to the field and climbed through the gap in the hedge.

The light from the house was hardly enough to see by, but Elfie groped in the weeds until she found Shonna's trowel, which was still there from the year before, rusty but usable. It took a long time to dig a hole big enough, even though the earth was soft from the summer rain. Gently, Elfie laid the bundle close to where she remembered burying the rose, and scooped the loose soil back over it, patting it down softly with the trowel. Now no one would ever know. It would be her last secret with Shonna.

Elfie stood up and looked down, brushing the mud from her knees. Would it be wicked not to say a prayer? She put her hands together and took a deep breath. Why was it when she knew so many prayers, they had all left her, and the only thing that came into her mind was 'The Little Peach'? She had had such trouble with it and now the last verse was the only thing she could remember. Elfie's voice fought its way out past the lump in her throat:

> 'Under the turf where the daisies grew,
> They planted John and his sister Sue.
> And their little souls to the angels flew.
> Boo hoo!'